A Father's Love

By
Steven Manchester

PublishAmerica
Baltimore

First printing

ISBN: 1-4137-0564-2
PUBLISHED BY PUBLISHAMERICA, LLLP
www.publishamerica.com
Baltimore

Printed in the United States of America

For Evan, Jacob, Carissa & Baby Manch

Aunt Jenna —

I hope you enjoy
these two tales support!

Thank you for your

With Love —

2013

Acknowledgments

First and forever, Jesus Christ- my Lord and Savior.
With Him, all things are possible.

Paula- the absolute love of my life.
My sons, Evan and Jacob, who share the best part of my heart.
Carissa- my friend and constant source of inspiration.
Mom, Dad, Billy, Randy, Darlene, Jenny, Celia and Philip
– my beloved family.
My mentor and dear friend, Russell N. McCarthy.

Special thanks to Keith Drab – my editor and friend.
Also, Shelley Bernardo, Cathy Nichols & Paula Kennedy – whose
early critiques turned *A Father's Love* into a much better read.

In no particular order:
Dan and Carol Calis, Rob and Julie Letendre, Patrick J. Barry,
Mark Grocholski, Rene and Karen Charest, Frank D'Agostino,
Barry M. McKee, Ken Weiss, Matt and Cheryl Olivier, Lou
Matos, Nelson and Tina Julius, Brad and Lisa Cowen, Lynn
Stanton, George Cournoyer, Al and Sandi Correiro, Manny and
Shelley Bernardo, Tom and Ana Thompson, Paul and Tonia
Patricio, The DeSousa Family, "The Dream Team" of Operation
Desert Storm, my brothers at SECC, Anita, Cathy, Coley, Fred
and friends at SSB, and all those my poor memory has failed…

My life has been richly blessed for
having known each one of you!

Foreword

It is usually impossible to separate a story from the person who wrote it. The craft is such an emotional venture that the author's feelings, soul, and overall being are unmistakably transferred onto the pages being written. Even the most skillful artisans who vow to write "out of character" leave traces of themselves in the words they scribe.

One would think that after having written the above, I am about to explain how Steven Manchester is somehow different; how he can become a different writer at any time and leave no trace of himself on the paper.

Actually my thoughts are quite the contrary.

Steven Manchester writes exactly what is in his heart and soul at all times, and that is why he is so talented. He consistently states, *"I can only write what I know."* Knowing him as I do, however, I know that this isn't entirely true, and is more a means of remaining humble. Writing what he feels in his heart is his strength. And writing what he knows without any pretense of trying to be different is what makes *A Father's Love* so moving. This is a work that is clear and pristine and direct from the heart. At several places in these twin tales, the author seems to allow a direct path from heart to pen. The results are words that are not slowed by thought or calculation, but flow onto the page directly from his emotional core.

A Father Love's is deeply moving *because* Steven Manchester "only writes what he knows." His stories are about life and the emotions that run through it. I'll paraphrase the words of a kind sea captain to describe the feelings that swing back and forth like a pendulum through these tales. *Challenge is paired with triumph, love is tied to despair, and through all of it runs a deep emotion.*

Read *A Father's Love* as Steven Manchester has written it, with an open heart. Enjoy.

Keith R. Drab
April 11, 2003

5

Part I
Three Shoeboxes

"How can someone take something from you when it lives in your heart?"
— Butch Pereira

~ I ~

Times were tight, really tight. Nevertheless, Tracey had been surprised with a diamond bracelet the year before. "I knew I should have waited the year," Dennis cursed himself. "I'm going to be making payments for the next five anyway."

As far as being creative or original, Dennis knew he wasn't going to top Christmas. He'd gotten Tracey a beautifully detailed black and gold chest, and filled it with a pile of gift-wrapped treasures. He started with a simple poem he'd written her, framed it and placed it on the bottom. It read:

More Than Words

"How much do you love me?"
she asked before she sighed.
And when I peered into her face,
I felt that I might cry.

Her hair was curls of chocolate;
her lips, a sweet dessert.
In her touch, I found my soul-
she felt so good it hurt.

A smile that men would die for,
she offered it to me.
Her laugh was so contagious,
it set my troubles free.

Her words were more than gentle;
her whispers, more than fun.
A mix of lust and innocence,
she soothed me like the sun.

She smelled of summer breezes
on golden fields of wheat.
I swear she had an aura
from her halo to her feet.

Yet, only when I searched her eyes,
the answer could be found .
I tried my best to tell her...
but never made a sound.

Although it took weeks, Dennis stuffed the box with her favorite music, some massage oils, perfume, chocolate and English tea. He added incense, some sexy lingerie, assorted lotions, candles, bubble bath and wine. In the space left, he placed a stuffed teddy bear holding a gift certificate for a professional massage. As the finishing touch, he took ordinary index cards and with a few magic markers and a little red ribbon, made her a "lovers" coupon book. Promises like *I'll cook dinner* and *Extended foot massage* were mixed in with more provocative freebies. Each could be cashed in at any time and were redeemable with only he. She absolutely loved it. Remembering her face, he just knew he'd be hard-pressed to get the same reaction again.

Dennis abandoned his mind and ventured off to his heart, where hopefully, the answer to his quest would be found. It didn't take long for the only obvious choice to hit him. He would give Tracey an experience rather than the usual material token. For their 10-year wedding anniversary, he would give her a memory.

He awoke earlier than she, as he had for the better part of a decade. Sitting up, he took the few precious moments needed to realize how much he really loved her. Though he'd memorized it years ago, he studied the soft contours of her face, eventually locking onto her full lips. Her smile stole away his yawn. Her smell was so sweet, so distinct. It was another of her details that he'd recognize in either heaven or hell. She stirred and began struggling to open her eyelids. He never budged, and was inches from her face when her senses registered his presence. "Happy Anniversary," he said. She purred once and pulled him to her. They hugged for a long while.

"I love you," she finally whispered in his ear.

He squeezed her tighter. After ten wondrous years, he was thinking the same exact thing.

As usual, he dressed and started for work. He apologized for having to work late at the firm on their anniversary.

"I understand," she promised. "We need the money."

He nodded. "We'll celebrate this weekend. We'll get a babysitter and go out."

She smiled, kissed him again and watched him hurry out the door. He unlocked the car door, slid behind the steering wheel and looked back the house. *What a trooper,* he thought, *wearing the bright smile the way she did.* But she was disappointed and he knew it. After ten years, even the best acting wouldn't have fooled either of them.

Four hours elapsed before the young messenger rang the Anderson's doorbell. He searched the side of the house for confirmation on the address and looked more stressed than anyone delivering flowers should have been. The bouquet was lovely. There were ten long stem roses, one for each cherished year. Tracey had asked that Dennis not send them. They could have used the money elsewhere. She was never so happy, though, that he'd ignored her wishes. She plucked the card free. It read: *Thank you for 10 great years, 3 beautiful children and 1 incredible life!*

Her smile lasted until the moment Dennis returned home.

"We have dinner reservations," he said with a wink. "You have a half hour to get ready."

She hugged him. "I love you," she whispered again in his ear. "But a half hour?"

He laughed. "Hurry," he said, adding a pat for her backside. "The kids are at your Mom's, so we have all night." He smiled. "So hurry!"

Nearly one hour later, they pulled up to D'Avios. It was a fancy restaurant located at the bottom of the posh Biltmore Hotel in Providence. The young valet attendant opened Tracey's door. In one swift motion, he caught Dennis's keys, along with a promise for a good tip. "I'll get you on the way out," Dennis said, and then grabbed his wife's hand to escort her into the restaurant. Curiously enough, he was holding a paper bag.

The ambiance was perfect, the service reached beyond doting, yet neither of these could compare to the meal. The steak melted like ice cream in July. They'd just ordered coffee and dessert when the pianist stopped playing and made an announcement. "I'd like to ask everyone to join me in wishing Mr. and Mrs. Dennis Anderson a happy anniversary. Ten years ago today, they took each other as man and wife, and we're honored to have them celebrating with us tonight." There was applause. With her mouth half hung from shock, Tracey looked across the table to catch the blush of a little boy paint her considerate husband's face. Before she could say a word, though, the pianist broke into his next song. It was their wedding song. Her eyes filled with tears. "Thank you," she whispered past the lump in her throat. "I…"

He leaned across the table and grabbed her hand, interrupting her emotional words. "Happy Anniversary, Babe." he said, and then revealed a wrapped present. "This gift is the one thing that means the most to me in the whole world." He handed it over to her.

While the pianist filled the room with nostalgia, she tore through the wrapping. In one magical moment, she reached the prize. It was a framed photo of them and the kids, Shane, Beth and Tyler. It was a picture of their family. "Oh God, do I love you," she cried and hurried over to kiss him.

He hugged her tight. "Good. So, I get another ten years?"

She never answered. Her embrace said it all. It was the best memory anyone had ever given her.

The following morning, Dennis gave Tracey another precious gift by allowing her to sleep in. She held down the Anderson fort each and every day, and deserved a break. He fed the kids and took them to the park. It was just another ordinary day that he'd cherish forever.

On the ride, he realized that he'd become so busy with imaginary deadlines that he'd forgotten the blessings of innocent fun. It had been awhile since he'd taken Shane, Beth and Tyler to the park. He peered in the rear-view mirror and smiled. They were all squirming from excitement.

As soon as they pulled in front of the park, the adventure began. With shoes unlaced, only their breathing could chug faster than their feet. Each one beat Dennis to the bottom of the hill. They were small, but they were quick.

While the kids headed for the swings, Dennis said hello to the other adults on supervision patrol. Most offered a grin, a nod, or a heavy sigh, and then quickly returned to the army of small children who attacked the jungle gym without mercy. Dennis took a seat and tried to get comfortable on the hard green bench, opting to do some people watching. He'd made fewer choices in his life that had turned out better.

As he sat on that bench and watched his children play, he realized something priceless. All the times he thought they weren't watching he and Tracey, they had been, and the examples were clearly paying off. All three of their children were genuinely good people – selfless and kind. He choked back the tears of pride.

While Shane and Tyler looked on, Beth approached. "Will you play with us, Dad?"

Dennis shook his head in disbelief. With all the kids running around, they actually wanted him to play with them. He stood and followed them.

As they stepped through the park, Dennis decided to forget himself and everything he knew as an adult.

At first, they tackled the slides, but that was only a warm-up.

From there, it was on to the real games. Like wild gorillas, they hit the jungle gym hard. Before long, the air turned hot. While playing hide-and-seek, Dennis's big butt and Beth's giggles gave them both away. Shane picked the game of tag next, and it was complete, unadulterated fun. Each of them laughed, really laughed and meant every second of it. There were no adults there to tell them what they couldn't do. They were royalty and knowing this, they quickly claimed their territory. They built a fort under the jungle gym.

Resting on a floor of dirt and wood chips, Beth made a birthday cake out of mud. She and her brothers sang out of tune, while Dennis blew out the candles. Then, to Dennis's surprise, Tyler found it. It was a treasure, the most valuable thing on earth: a bottle cap. "It's a real treasure!" the little guy squealed. "Let's bury it for some other lucky kids to find thousands of years from now. What a treasure!"

Quietly digging a hole, all four buried their treasure where nobody would ever find it. Dennis marked the spot with a stick, while they promised each other that they'd tell no one. It was their secret, something they could rediscover at their next visit to the park.

The entire day was magical. Tyler told stories that made no sense. The four of them ate fast-melting ice cream and danced under the sun. For everyone's entertainment, Beth described each person that passed with great fictitious detail. One was a real princess. Another was an astronaut. They lied in the grass, rolled down a hill and looked up to watch big puffy clouds float by. They took turns pointing out the obvious pictures painted above. Shane reverted their attention to a colony of ants that worked hard, marching in a straight row, each carrying his fair share. They played so many games Dennis had forgotten.

As the sun reached its peak over the bay, Dennis took a much-needed breather on the bench. As he watched his children expend their last burst of energy, he decided that everything worth knowing was learned young, and understood by children. Lessons like playing fair, the reasons not to fight, and so on, were really all anyone ever needed to know. In fact, anything more than that complicated and confused life. He was so blessed for the sweet reminder; blessed with the rare opportunity to view what honestly meant anything in life. He was grateful.

Shane, Beth and Tyler Anderson were the wisest people he'd ever met. With messy hair and wrinkled clothes, they didn't care one bit about success or wealth. Their only job was to laugh all day, which kept them healthy. For the most part, they listened well, and in their innocent way, sought out the truth in everything. Their minds were sponges in search of right. Their hearts were pure, and they had no qualms about sharing them. In their eyes, there was peace, while their mouths spouted the kindest words Dennis had ever heard. They were usually polite and good, trying desperately to choose right over wrong. In their smiles, there was forgiveness and healing, and each of them was pretty much an open book when it came to their feelings. The word shame was never affiliated with their true emotions. They worried so much less than most and their sleep was sound. Dennis sometimes wondered if they actually understood the true secret to joy. Their only possessions in the world were hope and love, and for that, they thanked the Lord daily. Dennis felt blessed they were his children and his eyes filled with the love that gushed for them. He just knew they were destined to live wonderfully enriched lives. Their willingness to share and be kind would guarantee it.

Covered in sweat and dirt, Dennis and the kids took to the swing set for the last time that day. Shane, Beth and Tyler talked about their lives and Dennis listened because that's what real Dads did. Racing to the top of the hill, Dennis beat them back to the car, but looking back one last time, he realized that he'd just enjoyed one of the best days of his entire life. There had been nothing but laughter, but somewhere through it all, something very serious happened. He'd been reminded that he was still alive – alive to run and play and laugh. With a grin, he shook his head. His children had taught him that he still had much to learn. Some days, he honestly thought that they knew more than he.

On the ride home, he looked back in the rear-view mirror and made a wish. He wished that – throughout their lives – Shane, Beth and Tyler would remember the days when they had all the answers and generously shared them with busy adults who sometimes forgot the important things in life.

Dennis smiled and set his gaze back upon the road before them. He'd never miss the opportunity to take a walk through the park again. There were so many treasures that waited to be uncovered and rediscovered.

~ II ~

One year later...

Colorful balloons tied to the mailbox of the Anderson's colonial home blew in a soft summer breeze. The quaint New England street was filled with parked cars on both sides. In the backyard, Dennis stood on the deck, enjoying the company of he and Tracey's many guests. The devoted husband and father of three cooked enough hamburgers and hot dogs for a small army. Children ran and played games, each wearing pointy party hats; each taking turns chasing Mr. Duffy, a shaggy brown mutt, in and out of the house. Adults gathered amongst themselves in small groups, sipping fruit-garnished cocktails and pretending to pay attention to their screaming children. A stereo played upbeat music. Life was good, and everyone was celebrating these facts and not just the birthday of Dennis and Tracey's youngest boy, Tyler.

As a band of screaming children chased Mr. Duffy into the kitchen, on the wall, the calendar showed the words TYLER'S BIRTHDAY written in big bold letters. The date was August 24, 1995. Mr. Duffy led them into the living room where he ran in circles. On the mantle above the fireplace, family photos in mismatched frames smiled from behind spotless plates of glass. Dennis and Tracey's wedding picture was surrounded by photos of they and the kids: Shots taken at Disneyland, the beach, a picnic, New York City and the aquarium – just to name a few. Though the settings changed, the themes were all the same. The entire Anderson family was together and smiling.

Dennis wore an apron reading *Kiss The Cook*, and flipped another batch of charred burgers onto the plate of buns being held by his wife. Before Tracey turned to leave, he stole a kiss from her. In turn, she playfully stole a swig of his beer. "Hey, get your own," he teased.

She giggled and put the platter of burgers down to grab his

smiling face. "My dear, in case you've forgotten – everything that is yours is mine."

He wrinkled his nose in a display of playful disapproval. Tracey took the opportunity to kiss him again. She patted his backside, and he gave her a wink. "And I wouldn't have it any other way, Beautiful," he whispered.

As she walked away, at a comical screech, Dennis called out, "Okay kids, come and get it!"

The children stampeded toward the grill and lined themselves up for their food. Dennis teased each one, affectionately patting the heads of Shane, Beth and Tyler.

Tracey chuckled, and joined her mother and sister at one of the plastic patio tables.

Joyce Newman, her mom, was recently divorced from Tracey's dad and showed all the signs of newfound freedom. She was already inebriated. Jenn Newman, her bitter sister, was younger than Tracey, but had already experienced enough life to be thoroughly jaded.

"So, did your father even call to wish Tyler a happy birthday?" Joyce asked.

Tracey rolled her eyes. "Yes Mom, he called. He said he'd be by this week when the old windbag wasn't around."

Joyce's nostrils flared. Within seconds, a smile replaced her sour puss. It didn't take long to realize she was wrong to bring up her daughters' father.

Jenn sipped her cocktail. "For someone who swears she doesn't care Mom, you spend an awful lot of time talking about Dad."

Joyce sighed heavy. "Some habits are easier to break than others, I suppose." She shook her head. "To tell you the truth, girls, I'm not sure you can ever stop caring for someone – especially when you've shared a love as deep as mine and your father's." She smiled. "For now, though, it's a lot more fun to hate him."

The three women shared a wonderful laugh.

Tracey's eyes found Dennis at the grill. Her expression changed from humorous to concern. Her mother immediately picked up on it.

"Since it's confession time," Joyce prodded, "why don't you tell me what's bothering you?"

Tracey shrugged. "I don't know, Mom. I really shouldn't complain. It's just that something is different with Dennis. Ever since the car accident, he's been unusually quiet. It's been months now. The doctor said that with the exception of the scar on his chin, he was blessed to come out of such a brutal car wreck unscathed." She shook her head. "Maybe they didn't examine him close enough."

Tracey drifted back to that horrid night. She felt that something was wrong before the phone even rang. It was the hospital. "Mrs. Anderson," the nurse said, "your husband has been in an auto accident and asked me to call."

"Is he okay?" Tracey asked. She tried to conceal her panic.

There was a terrible pause. "He's been beat up pretty badly, but he's going to be fine." There was another pause. "He's very upset, though."

"I'll be right there!" She could feel his pain.

Tracey felt a chill and opened her eyes to find her mother and sister staring at her. She took a deep breath. "Dennis hasn't been his usual funny and attentive self. I try talking to him, but he always dodges any issue that's serious. He even has a problem with my returning to work this fall."

Joyce was taken aback. "But I thought you guys had a plan."

"We do...or did. The plan was to have me get back on the newsroom floor once Tyler hopped on the school bus. In fact, it was Dennis's idea and until recently, he supported the dream completely. I know he's had a lot of pressure at work lately." She shrugged again. "It must be work."

"Typical man," Jenn snorted. "Completely self-absorbed."

Tracey looked up. As if he'd overheard the conversation, Dennis looked over at her. She offered a big smile. He returned the loving gesture with a wink, but something was wrong. She could just feel it. Several men were huddled near him. The beer bottles were already starting to pile up near the grill.

Joyce took notice and quelled her daughter's fears. "Take it from me, Sweetie, men can be just as mysterious as us. I wouldn't worry yourself, though. Dennis is a good husband and even if you tried, you couldn't have picked a better father for my grandchildren. My advice is to just be patient. He'll come around. As long as there's communication, respect and trust, love will find its way out of any problem." She grabbed Tracey's arm. "I have to tell you, though, you also have to be sure that your husband's life doesn't completely consume all of you." She shook her head. "You see the problem with your father was that he…"

"Precisely!" Jenn added. "Any man who thinks he can just…"

As an intended interruption, Tracey stood, shook her head and bent to kiss her Mom. "Thanks for the advice, Mom." She looked toward her sister and chuckled. "And Jenn, you really do need to get a life."

Joyce laughed. While Tracey set off to tend to her guests, Jenn wrinkled her forehead in thought.

There was a good time had by all. Dennis got progressively intoxicated, but even so, he took charge of the children's games. He hosted several chaotic rounds of musical chairs and one nearly fatal game of pin the tail on the donkey.

Once the clown arrived, the big-shoed prankster performed magic tricks and twisted balloons into animal shapes. Dennis took it one step further and filled many of the balloons with water. Within seconds, each child was armed for battle. Their laughter turned to wondrous squeals, while the magic spilled through the yard and contagiously rubbed off on every adult in attendance. Before it was over, even Joyce Newman was soaked from head-to-toe. Tracey never stopped laughing.

As the sun dove for the horizon, Tracey lit the candles on Tyler's cake. She and Dennis stood arm-in-arm and joined their family and friends in a strong rendition. "Happy Birthday to you. Happy birthday to you. Happy birthday dear Tyler, Happy birthday to you."

To a round of applause, the grinning boy blew out six candles. Tracey and Dennis stole another kiss from each other.

Tyler was the baby of the family, though from his attitude, one would never know it. He silently loved being coddled and pampered, while for all-to-see, he chose to spend his days trying to outdo his older brother, Shane. With his father's dark hair and mother's light eyes, he was intelligent and just as stubborn as he was compassionate.

Tyler's older siblings, Shane and Beth, passed over a pile of gifts to the birthday boy.

At ten, Shane was an all-American boy. He was the spitting image of his father, with dark hair and eyes. He loved baseball, exploring the great outdoors, skateboarding and amassing a giant baseball card collection. He was a dare devil and a leader – having some difficulties following the suggestions of others. An absolute adult-pleaser, he went beyond any means to prove himself.

Beth was eight. Pigtails and Barbie dolls were just starting to lose their attraction. With her mother's chocolate curls and light eyes, she was 'Daddy's girl' and had a tough time sharing his attention with her Mom. She was a caring and sensitive soul, yet having two brothers around she hardly revealed it. She kept her dreams locked within where she could visit them any time of the day.

Tyler tore through miles of wrapping paper until he was sitting before a mound of new clothes and shiny toys.

Dennis approached his young son. With a proud smile, he handed the boy his last gift. Tracey beamed with the boy's anticipation. Tyler ripped through the wrapping and opened the box. He pulled out a small white sailor's hat.

"Dad," he squealed. "Does this mean…?"

"It sure does, Ty," Dennis pushed past the lump in his throat. "You're now an official crew member of the Anderson sailing team." He winked at his son. "We ship out first light tomorrow."

"YOO HOO!!!" Tyler wailed.

Applause echoed through the yard for the second time.

It was nearly ten o'clock when the last of family and friends dispersed. After three exhausted children were tucked in for the night, Dennis and Tracey returned to the back deck. One step out, and they looked at each other and laughed. It was as if an angry twister had passed through just hours before. Steamers and broken balloons covered the lawn. Cake frosting was smeared on the patio furniture.

While crickets chirped, they worked together to clean up. There was a comforting silence. Tracey yawned, causing Dennis to do the same. Exhausted, they laughed again. Tracey wanted to talk. Dennis, on the other hand, just wanted to finish and go to bed. There was an early wake-up call scheduled. He was taking the kids sailing.

"Ty sure made out like a bandit," Tracey yawned.

"Sure did. They all do," Dennis agreed. "It's funny. I was thinking the same thing – thinking about how blessed we are for our family and friends. I don't see the kids ever going without."

"Nope. But it's the other stuff that makes me feel blessed," Tracey said. "The way you play with them; how they laugh; the love our family showers them with."

Dennis smiled, and decided to take a seat and a break from the cleaning. "You know, Trace, I don't even remember what life was like without the kids. And I'm glad I don't. You?"

Tracey took a seat near him and with a kiss, gave her response. They sat together for a few brief moments. As Dennis stood to tackle the rest of the debris, though, Tracey struggled to find the words for the real issue at hand. After a deep breath, she took the plunge. "Well, looks like a couple more weeks and I can pick up where I left off with my career."

Dennis stopped and locked eyes with his wife. "What's that?"

Attempting confidence, she went on. "Come September, all the kids will finally be in school full-time and…"

Dennis shook his head dismissively. "Don't be silly, Trace. Summer isn't even over yet. Besides, we don't need the money."

He looked away and continued cleaning. Tracey was taken aback by the *silly* comment. The issue was easily dismissed, but only by Dennis. She couldn't believe it. He'd always been the one to champion her dreams of writing. Something was way off. For the moment, she decided to let it go and not risk ruining a perfect day.

After checking in on the kids, they headed to the master bedroom and changed. Dennis wore a pair of pajama bottoms, while Tracey threw on the matching top. They slid into bed.

"Babe, we really do need to talk about me returning to work," she whispered.

Dennis rolled over and landed on top of her where he kissed her passionately. Her heavy breathing and faint moans quickly changed the subject.

"You sure you really want to talk about work right now?"

Tracey didn't respond. She slid off her top and pulled Dennis to her.

The sun was yet to rise when Dennis turned the mini-van onto the highway. He juggled the steering wheel and a hot cup of coffee. Tracey was deathly afraid of water, so she stayed home. She'd nearly drowned as a child and could never face her fears of the water. This bothered Dennis – especially since his car accident. It didn't make sense that his logical wife couldn't get past it. He decided not to make an issue of it, though. He supposed some things were better left to be dealt with alone. Besides, he kind of liked the idea of sharing his passion for sailing with just his children. It was his favorite way to bond with them.

All three kids were wide awake for the early hour. Excitement covered their small faces. Tyler beamed the brightest. At six years old, he was finally permitted to embark on his first watery adventure.

The sun finally made its grand entrance. As the Andersons headed for the lake, trees flew by the window. Dennis began a chorus of songs.

"Row, row, row your boat, gently down the stream. Merrily, merrily, merrily, merrily, life is but a dream…"

He peered in the rear-view mirror, and a smile engulfed his face. Life really was a dream.

At the sailboat slip, the children donned their bright orange life vests. Dennis took a knee and spoke to them about safety. "Okay, guys, sailing can be a lot of fun, but it can also be very dangerous. Like everything else in life, you'll be fine as long as you show respect. Respect for the boat, for the water – and for me."

Three sets of wide eyes stayed glued on their teacher.

"I'm the Captain of this ship," Dennis continued, "so you must listen to everything I tell you out there. If you don't, somebody might get hurt." He searched their eyes. "So when I tell you to do something, don't question it. Just do it. We can always talk about it later. Okay?"

"We know, Dad," Shane and Beth replied in symphony.

With his most serious face, Tyler saluted Dennis. "Aye, Aye, Captain."

Dennis, Shane and Beth burst into laughter. Tyler maintained his intense demeanor.

Dennis assisted each child onto the boat. He untied the ropes from the slip, threw them onto the boat and jumped on.

It was a calm, sunny day, with only a few clouds bringing about slight winds. It was a perfect day for Tyler to break into sailing. The three children sat at the rear of the boat and listened attentively as Dennis worked the sails. After tying off a rope, he began pointing out animals foraging on the shore, birds gliding in the sky, and so on.

Dennis looked up to find Shane's face frozen in awe. The boy scanned the world around him and when his eyes finally met that of his father's, he wanted to describe what he was feeling, but couldn't articulate it. Dennis knew his children.

With a smile, he answered the question that his eldest son could not put into words. "It's the feeling of freedom. That's what you feel, Shane." After a thoughtful pause, he spoke to them all. "But guys, you don't need to feel happy or peaceful to feel free. Like everything worth living for, freedom lives right in here." Dennis pointed to his chest. He inhaled deeply to drive his point home. The kids followed suit. After a proud smile, he returned to working the main sail. The kids looked at each other and grinned. The deep breathing continued.

~ III ~

The emergency room doctor grinned. "I have great news," he reported. "We can't find any evidence of a heart attack." Dennis was confused, almost strangely disappointed. "It was probably just a panic attack," the man concluded and prescribed a sedative that would render Dennis more useless than the alleged attack.

No way, Dennis thought, and walked away with his face burning red.

The doctor shrugged. "These attacks are sometimes caused by the building tensions of everyday life. Anything could have triggered the attack." Dennis nodded, thinking, *It's a wonder it didn't happen years ago.*

Dennis appreciated the man's concern, but was more grateful that no one knew but he and the foolish man. He didn't buy the spiel, though. Dennis was a master of the corporate rat race. If anyone knew how to survive, it was he.

He rewound the nightmare in his head. He'd been sound asleep when he jumped up gasping for air, his heart drumming out of his chest. He didn't know what was wrong. He leapt out of bed and stumbled toward the bathroom. He couldn't breathe. He couldn't think. There was something horribly wrong and he needed help. He searched frantically for an enemy. There was none. He was alone. As he stared at the frightened man in the mirror, he didn't realize that he'd never be the same again. Miraculously, he held on and didn't call for Tracey.

With pains in his chest, a sweaty face and shaking hands, he honestly believed that he was standing at death's door. It was nearly morning, though, so he sneaked out of the house and rushed to the emergency room.

"It was probably just a panic attack," the doctor repeated with a grin, startling Dennis back into the present.

"I think you should go talk to someone," the medicine man suggested.

Dennis nodded. "I'll go see my primary care physician tomorrow."

"That's great," the man said, softly, "but I was thinking more along the lines of a therapist."

The problem's physical, Dennis screamed in his head, and quickly applied his false mask of strength. He'd been thinking the same thing, but when put into words the possibility was even more terrifying. He merely smiled and grabbed his coat to leave.

Dennis arrived at New Dimensions Advertising. As an executive at the top of his game, he maintained a neat appearance and an even-tempered demeanor. He was energetic, in control and one step away from a big promotion. An early meeting had been scheduled with his creative team. He walked in late, a tray of hot coffees in one hand and a box of donuts in the other.

"I know. I know. I expect everyone to be here on time, except for me, right?" Dennis kidded his handpicked crew. "Okay, now that we have that cleared up." He waited. Except for several chuckles over the donut box, there was no response. He went on. "Oh. Tyler wanted me to thank everyone again for their generous gifts." He smirked. "Well, everyone but Brian."

Brian was an entry-level consultant. His head snapped up from the box. White powder covered his open mouth. He was clearly confused by the comment.

Dennis laughed. "No, I'm sorry Brian. I have that wrong. Tyler loves the monster truck you gave him. I'm the one who has a problem with it."

Brian still couldn't respond. His mouth was stuffed with a powdered donut.

Dennis leaned in close to his young prodigy and winked. "My friend, NEVER EVER buy a child a toy that can scream louder than the child's father." There was a comical pause. "Trust me, when you have kids, you'll know what I'm talking about."

Brian's smile displayed his relief. There were three women and two men seated at the conference table, and each of them chuckled. From the look in their eyes, there was also a great respect for their boss. It was clear. Dennis Anderson was well liked by his people.

As everyone dove back into the donut box, concepts at different levels of development began flying around the room. Dennis controlled the flow, occasionally writing down some of the ideas.

Brian took the floor and looked toward Dennis. "I've done the legwork on this one, boss. The way I see it, Woodpine Furniture is competing with three major retailers, each one located within a ten-mile radius of the other. With such a concentration, they can't..."

"Compete?" Dennis asked. "I disagree. In fact, it's been my experience that a rising tide carries all ships."

Brian awaited an explanation. They all did.

Dennis chuckled. "It means that when people are looking for furniture, they'll shop around – especially if it's only a ten-mile radius, and we can use this knowledge to give our client the edge." Dennis's eyes drifted off into a creative world that few people ever got the chance to visit. "That's our ace, Brian. We'll monitor the other stores' advertising and turn it into our own."

Dennis's entire team sat in awe at his genius. It truly was an honor to work with the best. Brian cleared his throat. "Ingenious," he said. "Perhaps then, we should..."

Dennis's eyes glassed over and he began to drift.

Brian's voice turned to a drone. "Blah...blah...blah..." the aspiring executive reported.

Dennis realized his mind was floating away again, but this time wasn't promising a pleasurable experience. He couldn't help it. His breathing quickened and a bead of sweat formed on his brow. Aware of his lack of concentration and the fact that he couldn't stop squirming, he eventually stood and cleared his throat. "If you'll excuse me, please."

As he hurried out the room, Brian halted his informal presentation. There was shock, and hushed inquiries began traveling from one person to the next.

Dennis rushed to the management washroom. Before the door closed completely, he was already splashing cold water on his face and breathing deeply. As he tried to calm himself, he stared deeply into the mirror. "What is wrong with me?" he muttered to his frightened reflection. "Dear God, what is wrong with me?"

Fifteen miles, or a world away in the Anderson home, Tracey went through her daily routine with the kids. Just as breakfast was served, she broke up a quarrel that was turning physical between Shane and Tyler. To make matters worse, Beth was feeling left out and was getting clingy. While she longed for her mother's attention, the boys remained relentless. Tracey had finally taken enough. "Boys! I've just about had it with your fighting," she yelled. "School will be starting in another week and you won't have as much time to play together. I suggest that you make the most of the summer you have left."

Shane offered the first explanation. "But Tyler is always in my stuff, Ma."

"Na...ah," Tyler quickly countered.

"He is, Mom," Shane vowed.

"I've heard enough from the both of you," Tracey howled. "Now either get outside and find a way to get along, or go to your room where you can fight all day if you want. It's up to you." Her eyes were stern; her hands, placed upon her hips.

The boys knew she meant business, and there was quiet until Beth called for her attention. "Mom?"

As she turned to her little girl, the boys exchanged punches under the table. Tracey's head snapped back to them. That was it and they knew it. In seconds, they were running for the great outdoors. The hooting and hollering, however, stayed behind long after the screen door slammed shut. Tracey shook her head and turned to Beth. "Boys," she sighed. "What are we going to do with them?"

Beth never hesitated giving the only logical answer. "Let's just get rid of 'em."

Tracey's laughter replaced that of the boys. She bent and hugged her daughter.

Dennis was seated at his desk when the phone rang. He didn't answer. Instead, amidst the framed colorings of his children's artwork, he picked up a picture of his family. No sooner did he have both hands on it, there was a knock at the door. As the door slowly opened, he sat still, almost paralyzed. Jim Hancock, the agency V.P., stuck his head in. He was looking for a project update. "Dennis, have we brushed in the final touches on the Woodpine project?"

Dennis looked at his boss with a distant stare.

The wise man shut the door behind him and took a seat across from the best man he had. "Do you want to talk about it?" Jim asked.

Dennis shook his head. "Nothing to talk about. Brian has a few good ideas, but some bugs still need to be worked out. We're going to need another solid week."

"I wasn't talking about work."

Dennis looked at his boss with confusion until he remembered that Jim was also a friend; another friend that gave Tyler a loud screeching toy.

"I don't know, Jim," Dennis said. "I suppose I just feel a little run-down lately." He shrugged. "I can't really place my finger on it."

Jim squinted. The answer was a little fuzzy, but Dennis had always been a straight shooter. "Have you seen a doctor?"

Red-faced, Dennis shook his head. "Nah. I suppose I should, though. I haven't been since the accident. You know me with doctors."

Jim stood and turned to leave. "Dennis, make sure you get yourself looked after. In the meantime, no pressure." At the door, he smiled wide. "But the Woodpine proposal has to be in the bag soon, or the firm's going to lose more money than it can afford."

As Jim shut the door behind him, Dennis returned to his family photo. "Yeah Jim," he snickered. "No pressure." It seemed like everything in life was starting to make him sweat.

It was nearly one o'clock when Tracey pulled the mini-van into a McDonald's drive-thru. The kids each screamed their orders over the front seat. This quickly turned into them screaming at each other. Tracey placed the Happy Meal orders, and then spun to threaten her tribe into silence. Minutes later, three bagged lunches got passed from one window to the next. Tracey pulled the van up a few feet and stopped to check that the orders were correct. When she looked up, an old colleague, Marie Virtucci, was standing right in front of the van. Marie was a glimpse of Tracey's previous life.

Instinctively, Tracey attempted to avoid her old friend. It was too late. The older woman waved and started toward the van. Tracey cursed under her breath and hurried to fix her hair in the rear-view mirror. She shook her head at the lack of makeup. One mumbled curse later, Marie's face appeared in the window. Tracey took a big breath, put on her best smile and rolled down the window.

"Hey stranger," Marie teased, "there's been rumors that you actually fell off the face of the earth." She shot a toothy smile. "To tell you the truth, I was starting to believe them, myself."

"Oh no...not at all..." Tracey fumbled. She was at a complete loss for words. Her kids, however, were not. They started fighting over the Happy Meal toys. Tracey danced between an adult conversation and reprimanding her children. "Shane, get that fist out of your brother's face," she hissed. "NOW!"

"Mom, why does..." Beth began to ask.

Tracey raised her hand. "Beth, honey, Mommy's trying to have an adult conversation right now, okay?" While Tracey blushed with embarrassment, Marie smiled.

"It certainly looks like your plate is full, though," Marie said. She obviously judged Tracey's situation with condescension.

Tracey had begun her journalism career with Marie, a woman who was not as good, but now an editor. The truth of it left a bad taste in Tracey's mouth.

The tone of the conversation surprisingly changed. "I have to tell you, Tracey," Marie said, "I've seen very few who have a way with words the way you do. You really are one of the best." The new editor looked at the children. "You should think about going back and doing what you love. There's nothing wrong with balancing both. It might not be as fun as this." She winked. "But we'd love to have you back."

Tracey smiled and blew an unruly wisp of hair from her eyes. "Geez, Marie. I'll have to really think about it. Why don't I give you a call sometime next week?"

Marie picked up on the brush off. As she walked away from the van, she half-waved at the kids.

Tracey sat parked for a while, thinking about the great offer. The kids, however, took the opportunity to get started in on round three.

~ IV ~

Dennis returned home from work, disheveled and exhausted. The kids didn't take notice. Rather, they took turns smothering him in hugs and kisses.

"How was your day, Hon?" Tracey asked, trying to initiate a conversation.

He didn't answer. She waited for him to inquire about her day, but he never reciprocated the same concern. Instead, he grabbed a beer from the fridge.

"I saw Marie Virtucci today," Tracey continued. "She told me…"

Dennis was unknowingly self-absorbed. With distant eyes and a few simple nods of his head, he ignored her completely. Tracey stopped and watched as he drank heartily from the shiny can. It was very unusual for a weekday, but for the time being she decided to let it go.

"Come on, guys," Tracey yelled at the kids. "Dinner's ready."

A small stampede entered from the living room.

"Go wash your hands," she instructed her merry band. "All of you."

"We did," they sang.

"Then wash them again. And this time, use soap."

Throughout dinner, besides the bantering between the children, there was a strange silence. Dennis was in his own world, removed from the entire scene. No matter how she tried, Tracey just couldn't reach him.

She wiped her mouth and gazed at her husband. "Dennis? You want to tell me what's going on inside that handsome head of yours?"

"Sit on your bum at the table," he yelled at Tyler. A few seconds passed before he looked up at his worried wife. She was awaiting a reply. "I'm sorry, Babe. It's just work. We've got a big deal that has to be wrapped up soon. Either that, or we lose the client entirely and I start delivering newspapers for a living." He offered a weak smile.

She didn't know whether or not to buy his casual demeanor. "Well then," she replied, "it's a good thing Jim has you on the project." She returned the wink. "From what I hear, thirty five year-old newspaper boys are a dime a dozen."

Dennis's smile was even weaker than before, leaving her at a complete loss. She really didn't know what to think. She rushed the children to finish dinner. He hardly noticed.

Once the dishes had been dried, the Anderson clan retired to the family room where they went through their normal nightly routine. Tracey picked up a book. Dennis clicked on the TV. And the kids played a board game until they could no longer interact peacefully. As the bickering got loud, Dennis exploded. "That's enough," he roared. "Put it away!"

His tone was sharper than usual. The kids froze in place.

He caught it and lowered his tone. "If you think you can behave, you can watch TV with me and Mom. If you can't do that, then you can all go to bed."

Tracey closed her book and gave the kids a look that said it all. It wasn't a good night to test Dad. They quickly did as they were told. A short time passed before she carted them off to bed. Each stopped at their Dad's recliner to kiss him goodnight. Dennis's attitude changed from cranky to loving. Tracey made a mental note of the sudden swing. Something was definitely wrong. He was getting unusually short with the kids.

Beth, the last of the kissing patrol, grabbed his face. "Daddy, I hope you have a better day tomorrow," she whispered. "Cause I really love ya and I hate when you're sad."

"Thank you, Princess. And I really love you, too."

Tracey escorted their sweet daughter off. Dennis looked ready for tears.

Tracey returned to the family room. "Ready for bed?" she asked her puffy-eyed husband.

Dennis followed her into the bedroom. While she stepped into the

34

bathroom to get changed, he stripped to his underwear, turned on the TV and sat at the edge of the bed, entranced. Tracey quickly returned, looked at the TV and took a seat beside him.

"Alright now, you want to tell me what's going on?"

He stared at the TV. She grabbed the remote, turned off the set and stood before him. He gazed up, almost catatonically. "It's nothing, Babe."

"Fine," she barked. "Since you want to shut me out of your life, let's talk about what's going on in mine."

Dennis's stomach flopped. He didn't want to shut her out. He felt he had no choice.

Tracey stared at him for a long time. "I've tried to figure out what's eating at you, Dennis. I swear I have. I've asked again and again, but it's never a straight answer." She paused. "If you want to lock me out, then there's nothing more I can do."

"Trace," he mumbled, "I think my creative juices have dried up on me." This explanation surprised Dennis even more than Tracey. He'd never failed at work, and couldn't understand why he feared it now.

Tracey abandoned her train of thought and focused on her husband's fears. "Don't be silly," she blurted. "You're the best in the business. I know it. You know it. And everyone else knows it."

Dennis offered a half-smile for her encouragement.

She hugged him, and then whispered playfully into his ear. "And I'm not sure you remember, but work isn't the only thing you're good at."

His eyes had already drifted off. "Huh?" he asked. "What?"

Tracey said nothing. A heavy sigh was her only proof of frustration.

Dennis caught it. "I'm sorry," he muttered. "I just had an idea." He jumped up and headed for the door, leaving his wife half-naked and alone. "If I don't write this stuff down now, I might lose it."

"Go. Get to work," she said, hiding her disappointment with an equal amount of support.

As he left, she slid up in the bed, pulled her knees to her chest and stared at the empty pillow beside her. A dramatic sigh followed her husband down the stairs.

In the quiet of the late hours, Dennis nodded off in his recliner. Three winks later, he flew from the chair and nearly yelled for help. Within seconds, he fell into a heap, horrified by a world of darkness that only he could see. He began to cry, and tried to hold on, exerting more will than he'd ever mustered. He was certain he wasn't going to make it to the hospital alive. The feeling that he was going to die washed over him like a heavy acid shower. He felt his entire existence, his very essence plunge into a freefall. While his sweaty, trembling hands gripped the telephone receiver; he tried desperately to catch his breath – contemplating an ambulance ride. He tried all he could to slow both his heart and thoughts. It was no use. He could feel the damage scar his very core. He was in trouble. Then, five eternal minutes later, it was over. Exhausted, he collapsed back into his chair. Though he might have been afraid to close his eyes again, he was happy and proud that he never made the call. Grateful that Tracey and the kids didn't know, he wiped the tears from his eyes.

He now knew it was going to happen the next day, and again and again, and the symptoms were going to grow more relentless each time. Life was getting unbearable. Like a predator in the darkest night, fear stalked nearby. Hours of blissful slumber were replaced by the most demented reality. The nightly attacks were a rough, intense experience, testing him each time to his limits and beyond. While the rest of the world peacefully snored away, he feared blinking for too long. Living was starting to give way to basic survival, while any nightmares he now experienced were his actual life. His mind longed to flee from itself.

Am I going crazy, or is this some angry disease spreading through my body? he thought.

Tracey stirred at the first light and looked up at her husband. Dennis's eyes betrayed a night of lost sleep. He sat at the edge of the bed and stared off into space. His hair was still wet from the shower.

She emerged from her slumber and wiped the sleep from her eyes. "Get it done?"

He snickered, stood and started to dress.

She sat up. "Dennis, I really need to talk."

"Then talk."

"I've been thinking about Marie Virtucci's offer."

His voice never reached beyond indifference. "Again with Marie Virtucci? I thought we already decided…"

"No. We didn't decide anything," she barked.

"Trace, I have too much going on to argue."

"I'm not finished, Dennis. For once, just let me finish!"

With trembling hands, she scooted to the foot of the bed. For the first time in a long time, Dennis realized that his wife needed to be heard. It scared him. He wasn't a selfish man, but right now the last thing he needed were more issues to deal with. He sensed it was absolutely crucial that life stay as it was – at least until he figured out what was going on inside of him. The very thought of change terrified him.

She spoke slowly. "As much as you think my life rotates around only you, I still have my own dreams."

"I'm sorry, Trace," he interrupted. "But…"

"DENNIS, PLEASE!" she screamed.

He shut up.

Reluctantly, she started to speak again, but couldn't. The tears would not allow it. Instead, she headed for the bathroom and closed the door behind her.

Feeling regret and sorrow, Dennis finished getting dressed and yelled through the door. "Hon, please don't be upset. We'll figure something out. But I've got to get to the office." He placed his hand on the door. "We'll talk when I get home, I promise. Okay?" Besides the start of another panic attack, he was already running late for his secret doctor's appointment.

Once Tracey heard the front door close, she came out of hiding. With one look around, she released a terrible screech.

Oblivious to her husband's difficult plight, Tracey went through her morning chores. The kids destroyed the kitchen with breakfast before their voices spilled through the screen door. As if she expected it to ring, Tracey stared at the phone. She finally picked up the receiver and dialed. "Hi. Marie Virtucci, please?"

Dennis sat at his own trusted physician. "There's no evidence of heart trauma," Dr. Lauermann concurred upon returning to the examining room. "It was probably just anxiety."

Just? Dennis vowed right then to be strong. No matter how bad it got, he wasn't going to any more doctors. It was his dark, little secret and he was determined to manage it alone.

He rolled out of the parking lot in his Lexus and started up the road. Throwing on his sunglasses, it didn't take long to pick up his cell phone and punch in the number to work. "Mornin' Sue. It's Dennis. Would you please let Jim know that I won't be in today. Seems my little guy gave me a touch of an early bug." There was a pause. "Right. I'll call him later. Okay, bye."

He hung up and pulled a U-turn toward the highway that led directly to the lake.

Within one hazy moment in time, he was set adrift on the lake. Seated in the fetal position, tears streamed down his face. Life was anything but a dream.

In such a short period of time, Dennis's internal battles had gotten even worse – until they actually melted into his daylight hours. More vicious than any adversary, the rubbery legs, lightheadedness, cold sweats and nausea commanded his days. He quickly learned to fear the attacks to come even more than those he experienced at the time.

He became intimate with the absolute terror of it all. The physical and mental toll was excruciating. There was a constant feeling of doom and gloom, of utter despair. Each sudden impact was all consuming. It seeped into every aspect of his life and threatened to ruin him socially, career-wise, and financially. He tried to sever the feelings by drinking, but it was merely a band-aid. It helped momentarily, but always came back the next day with a bitter vengeance.

Without truly knowing how he got there, Dennis sat on a barstool at Bobby's Lounge. The interior of the place was dimly lit. Bobby Lepage, owner and barkeep, was wiping down glasses behind his bar. A talk show, dancing in and out of static, played on the tube. Bobby shook his head at Dennis, who was already wrestling with his fourth drink. The clock read 12:45 p.m. The bar was empty. Dennis was slouched over, the world completely resting on his shoulders. It was tragic. Although anxiety was the cause, alcoholism had become one of its effects. The disease had weakened him.

"Wanna tell me about it?" Bobby asked.

Dennis slammed his glass on the bar, making Bobby's eyes go wide. "Everybody's a therapist," he hissed. "Why don't we just talk about another drink, okay?"

Bobby shook his head again, this time for Dennis to see. He poured another one, left the bottle and swiped Dennis's twenty-dollar bill off the bar. "Knock yourself out, partner."

While the large man returned to his spotted glasses, Dennis gulped the whiskey.

The telephone was on its fourth ring before Tracey grabbed it. She was panting from chasing the kids around out back. "Hello?"

"Hi Tracey. It's Jim Hancock."

"Hi Jim," Tracey replied. "And I recognized the voice. What's up?"

"I need to talk to Mr. Hookie for a minute."

"Mr. Hookie?"

"Yeah. Dennis. Could you put him on. I have a quick question."

Tracey's face went flush. There was an awkward moment of silence, allowing her time to think. "Actually…Jim…" she babbled. "Dennis stepped out for a moment. Should I have him call you when he gets back?"

Jim picked up on the confusion and quickly put the puzzle together. His tone changed from playful to disappointed. "No. Just tell him to come and see me first thing tomorrow morning."

Tracey hung up the phone in shock. A thousand bad scenarios played out in her head. With trembling hands, she picked up the receiver again and punched in some numbers. "Mom? It's me. Dennis didn't go to work today." There was a pause. "No. He never said where he was going. I think he might be having an affair." The tears were already starting to fall.

The entire day was spent ping ponging between terrible worry and unsubstantiated anger. She felt waves of fear so deep within her core that several times she thought she was going to vomit.

A week fit itself into a day before Dennis returned home intoxicated. It was well past dusk, but enough natural light remained to show a dent on the left front fender of the Lexus. Tracey was waiting on the doorstep, her arms folded across her heaving chest. Worry gave way to pure rage. As Dennis approached the stairs, her voice shook terribly. "You had me worried sick," she managed.

He attempted to walk past her. She halted him at the door.

"You stink like booze," she hissed. "Where've you been?" No matter how hard she tried, the tears kept building. "And – who've you been with?"

"Don't be crazy, Trace," he slurred. "I needed some time to myself, so I went to the lake. I had a few drinks at Bobby's."

She stormed into the house. He staggered in behind her. The kids were in the family room, a terrible concern swimming in their eyes. Tracey spotted them and headed for the master bedroom. As the door slammed shut, she wailed, "WHO DO YOU THINK YOU ARE – COMING HOME LIKE THIS? You told me this morning that we'd talk when you got home from work. Then, Jim Hancock called."

Dennis could hardly stand. "To hell with Jim Hancock," he burped.

"Oh, that's real nice, Dennis."

He collapsed onto the bed. His mouth was hung open, his eyes flitting in and out of consciousness.

She began crying uncontrollably. "This is just great, Dennis," she stuttered. "Swear to me that you haven't been with another woman. GO AHEAD, SWEAR IT!"

"What's the matter with you?" he slurred again, "accusing me of foolishness like that? I'd never even think of messing around on you. I love you, Trace." There was an awkward pause. "It's just that I...I...feel sick."

Tracey was at the door when she cut off his babble. "You should feel sick, Dennis. You've been drinking all day."

"No," he whispered. "You don't understand."

Shaking her head, she opened the door, looked over her shoulder and told him, "Sure, Dennis. I never understand." Switching her tone to condescension, she rolled her eyes. "If you do decide to go to work tomorrow, Jim wants to see you first thing in the morning. And you might want to get an estimate on the fender you dented." She paused again and then let him have it. "Oh, and I talked to Marie Virtucci today. I'm interviewing tomorrow for a reporter's position at the paper."

He sprung up in bed. She never noticed and slammed the door behind her. He collapsed back onto the bed, placed his hands over his eyes and let out a wounded grunt.

~ V ~

Dennis looked like death warmed over, while Jim Hancock looked like he'd been assigned as Death's own messenger.

"Dennis, I have no idea what's happening in your personal life," Jim began, "but I'm warning you now: Take care of it before it destroys your professional life."

Dennis nodded. He wanted to explain. Jim was steamed, though, and couldn't have cared less at the moment. Dennis stood and started for the door. As he reached the threshold, Jim finished, "And no more stalling on the Woodpine project. I want it completed by Friday, or you're off the account. No more excuses."

Again, Dennis only nodded. With one simple sigh, he exited, leaving Jim completely befuddled.

Tracey was dressed in a red power suit for the newspaper interview. She was visibly nervous, but firing the answers back as fast as they were being asked. Joe Bigelow, the editor-in-chief, fingered through her thick portfolio. He was thoroughly impressed. Marie Virtucci was in attendance. Everyone was smiling.

"I have an investigative reporting position available," Joe said. "When can you start?"

Tracey's eyes grew wide. "The kids begin school in a week. I can start just as soon as I see them on the bus."

Joe stood and extended his hand. "Well then, welcome aboard."

Tracey shook his hand. "Mr. Bigelow, thank you so much for this opportunity. I promise you won't be sorry." She was finally back in the game, and beamed at the truth of it. Suddenly, she felt a sharp pang of fear and wondered how Dennis was going to react. Within seconds, the sensation subsided. Dennis had always supported her decisions and would understand.

Halfway across the city, Brian sat across from his boss. Dennis was hung-over and spoke in hushed tones. "I've been thinking,

Brian. I really feel that you're ready for your first big test in the ad business."

Brian smiled. He didn't understand.

"I like your ideas on the Woodpine Project," Dennis explained. "And I'm prepared to let you run with it. You know, prove yourself, so to speak."

Brian slid to the edge of his seat, excited.

Dennis stood. "So, I'll expect the preliminary package by tomorrow evening, and the finished proposal by Friday afternoon." After a wounded smile, he used his remaining energy to raise an eyebrow. "Think you can handle it?"

Brian leapt to his feet. "Consider it done!" He rushed off to get started, but stopped dead at the door. "Want me to keep this between us?" he asked.

Dennis appreciated the loyalty, but cringed at the evidence of everyone knowing there was something wrong with him. "No," he answered. "This is my call."

Brian shrugged. "Okay, Boss. Thanks for the shot. I promise you won't be sorry."

As Brian left, Dennis placed his head on his desk and moaned. His brain felt like it might actually implode.

Mr. Duffy was the only one home when Dennis stepped through the front door. The house was empty. There was a note on the table. *Shane has a dentist's appointment and then we're going shopping for school clothes. I'll bring home take-out.* The note wasn't signed and there wasn't a hint of love in one single letter.

Dennis fed the dog before taking a strange tour of his house. As if he'd never seen the place, he studied photos of the children, colorings on the fridge, and other things he'd forgotten to miss. He grabbed a beer, and as he headed into the living room he noticed the answering machine flashing. He pushed the button. It was Marie Virtucci's voice. "Tracey, just confirming that the interview has been scheduled for 12:00. Joe thought it was strange to schedule it during lunch, but I didn't even get into the child care concerns."

There was a short pause. "But I did tell him that you were the best I ever worked with. I think it's in the bag. See you at the interview."

"You've got to be kidding me?" Dennis groaned. Mr. Duffy never answered.

It was well past dusk when Tracey and the kids returned home. Beth and Tyler were yelling at each other. Shane was quiet, his mouth swollen. Tracey fumbled with bags of groceries and a massive tub of fried chicken. Dennis grabbed the bags from her and awaited a kiss. It didn't come.

"When were you going to tell me?" he asked.

"Tell you?" Tracey looked surprised. "Tell you about what?"

"About the interview at the paper?"

She rolled her eyes. "I've been talking about returning to work for weeks, Dennis. It's just that you haven't heard a word I've said – for weeks!" She quieted her tone. "I had actually planned on having a quiet night together."

He turned his back to her and started for the kitchen. She rolled her eyes again and instructed the children to wash their hands for dinner. She couldn't believe it. For years, she'd managed the house and raised the kids, and when it finally came time for her to find success outside the home, her husband chose the role of obstacle. She could have screamed.

Even at the kitchen table, they couldn't conceal their anger for each other. There was no hiding it. The termite of miscommunication had taken another nasty bite. Dennis felt desperate. "We need you here," he finally blurted.

"No Dennis," she squealed. "I'VE BEEN HERE. NO MORE! Besides, the kids will be in school while I'm at work." She glared at him. "I think it's about time we share the responsibilities at home. For the past ten years, I've done it all."

He stood, threw his chair under the table and stormed off, leaving her shaking her head. Tracey was right, but the idea of her leaving the home now caused panic in his heart.

Tracey had thought about it and decided that even without Dennis's blessing, she was taking the job. The health of her soul depended on it.

There was silence. The kids squirmed with the realization that their parents were in the midst of a heated battle. Tracey soothed them. "Don't worry, guys," she said. "Daddy's under a lot of stress at work. He'll be fine."

They all looked at her with disbelief.

She shook her head in disgust. "Just finish your dinner."

The silence droned on.

Life in the master bedroom proved no different. Amongst a growing list of other things, Tracey was also finished initiating romance that Dennis constantly failed to return. She quickly fell asleep. Dennis, however, sat up in bed, preparing to face another bout with pain. She didn't know it, but long ago it had become a nightly routine. For the first time in Dennis's life, he felt alone.

Tracey awoke early to find Dennis already gone. She sat up and thought about how much he'd changed. As much as she was concerned, she was equally puzzled. Dennis was falling apart right before her eyes, but the reasons for this remained invisible to the eye. She'd never felt so frustrated and scared her whole life.

On his ride to work, Dennis also pondered how much he'd changed. Oddly enough, daily stressors weren't factors at all. In fact, he was so wired all the time that he actually felt comfortable under duress. When he was at ease, though, the world began to unravel. He couldn't breathe, swallow or walk. If he were sitting still, he'd suddenly want to jump up and flee from some invisible enemy. If he were in a public forum, he'd quickly sense the walls close in around him and fear lashing out. Even on his knees in prayer, he felt at danger. He often found himself alone in the living room, drinking scotch and wondering when and if his courage would ever return. On many nights, he thought about letting Tracey know, but decided against it. The shame of being perceived a 'nut job' was more painful than the torment he suffered alone.

The next few days whipped by in a blur. On Saturday, the last family outing of the summer was planned for the zoo. In the thick heat, Dennis and Tracey remained frigid to each other. The kids picked up on it and left them alone.

Every animal from the three-toed sloth to the white tiger was visited. While Dennis took the time to explain and discuss each species, Tracey took charge of the picture taking and snacks. Toward the end of their concrete safari, Shane noticed one of the animal trainers standing inside the lion's cage.

"Hey, look!" the excited boy called out. "That guy's standing right near the lion and he isn't even afraid."

Dennis placed his arm around his son. "Now that's a brave man, huh? I bet if you wanted to be, Shane, you could be a lion trainer when you grow up."

Shane shook his head. "No, Dad," he said with conviction. "When I grow up, I wanna be just like you."

Taken aback by the sincerity in his young son's voice, Dennis's eyes watered. As Tracey and the kids walked away from the lion's cage, Dennis looked up one last time. "No, Shane," he whispered under his breath. "You can do a lot better than that."

The newspaper read September 21, 1995. Tracey glowed over her first published by-line since returning to journalism. Joe Bigelow passed by and commented, "It didn't take you long to keep your promise, Tracey. Great piece on the Board of Health. I'm not sure they appreciate it, but I do. It's a fine piece of journalism."

Tracey glowed brighter.

Marie Virtucci patted her on the back, while Pete Loban, the newspaper's photographer, joined in on the celebration. "You've even made me look good," Marie whispered. "I'm buying lunch."

All four grabbed their jackets and headed off to the local bar and grille. Even with all the excitement, Tracey couldn't wait to get home and share her success with Dennis.

It was almost five before she finally arrived home – smiling like a kid at Christmas. Her jacket wasn't even off when she showed Dennis the article. He read it and patted her arm. "Nicely done. Congratulations," was all he could say. His words echoed with emptiness.

She was crushed. If he'd been any more excited about her small success, he would have been sleeping. What she didn't realize, however, was that he was so consumed with worry over his own life and the mounting pressures at work, that he was blind to anything else. She didn't know that he was petrified of the many dangers his own existence now faced.

During dinner, she initiated a conversation, but never asked about Dennis's day. Instead, she spoke of her own and of the incredible photographer whom she'd been assigned with. "Pete's work is the best I've ever seen," she boasted. "He's got such a way of expressing himself and his passions."

Dennis shot her a dirty look.

"What?" she asked.

He ignored her and turned to his son. "Come on, Shane. Get out your homework. Dad'll help you."

Tracey threw a dishtowel across the kitchen and rushed out of the room. Instinctively, Dennis stood and started after her, but was halted by his son. Though he felt bad, he merely shook his head and chose to take care of his boy. Even as he reclaimed his seat at the table, he knew it was the wrong choice.

~ VI ~

The morning had vanished with nothing to show for it when Dennis received a call at the office. As he struggled to maintain his composure and keep his job, Tracey informed him, "Dennis, I'm really behind on a deadline today. I need you to pick up the kids from school."

He gritted his teeth. Before he could speak, though, Tracey rattled off a list of places to transport the kids. She wasn't asking and it made him furious. "Shane is staying after for basketball practice," she explained. "Beth has to be at dance by four and Tyler usually gets a snack as soon as he gets home."

"You sure that's all of it, Trace?" he asked. "Cause God knows I've got nothing to do around here."

She was equally enraged. Her husband hadn't displayed one ounce of willingness to compromise. He obviously resented sharing her responsibilities. "Welcome to parenthood," she snickered, and hung up, leaving Dennis cursing her name.

He slammed the phone into its cradle and checked his watch. He was going to have to hurry to get the kids. "Damn it," he roared and sprinted out of the office.

Tracey was late getting home and there was no dinner on the table. Dennis cooked something nearly inedible, leaving everyone unhappy – even Mr. Duffy. The meal was so bad it had even the kids complaining about their mother's absence. After two cartoons, he tucked them into bed early.

Tracey arrived home to a house in darkness. Upon entering their bedroom, she found Dennis asleep. She would have never guessed he was pretending.

To the credit of his unbending will, Dennis stayed away from doctors until the symptoms grew more frequent and evolved into tingling extremities. Not even Dennis Anderson was a match for the

48

instant startle sensation. As if in imminent danger, the body froze and felt the need to flee, while two invisible anchors tied down the legs. Then, the symptoms came on fast and furious: heavy sweating, hyperventilation, spiraling thoughts of impending doom, nausea, twitching, tingling and tightness of the body, even a thumping heart that felt as if it randomly skipped a beat. Sitting white faced and alone each time, the intensity of the attack lasted five to ten excruciating minutes. Life was hell.

He finally confided in a friend and trusted colleague at New Dimensions Advertising. As he complained about Tracey not being there for him, Fred Beshara countered the attack. "What are you crazy, man? Your wife sacrificed everything to raise your kids."

Dennis felt ready for tears. He was falling apart. "I don't know what it is, Fred," he confessed. "I feel so different most of the time. There's nothing really wrong, nothing going on, but I'm down. I'm always down, and when I'm not, I feel like I'm having a heart attack."

"Go to counseling," Fred suggested. "It could be anxiety or depression. Maybe even both."

"Can't be," Dennis snickered. "Have you ever seen my kids...my beautiful wife? I got a great job, a nice home. Nope. I don't have time for anxiety or depression. Besides, I can't afford to have anyone know. My family's counting on me." The very suggestion terrified him. There were too many people counting on him. He couldn't scare them. It was a passing thing, and he'd just have to deal with it.

"But you can't afford to get worse," his friend said. "No one has to know."

Dennis agreed. The attacks were now happening two-to-three times each day. He fought back the fear, but it was becoming too much to bear. The violence of the attacks terrified him. He was broken in body, mind and spirit, or at least that's how he felt. He needed help. There was no more hiding it. If he didn't reveal the truth, there may not be a whole lot of him left. For the first time, he considered taking the risk of being labeled.

Fred reached into his wallet and pulled out a business card. He threw it on Dennis's desk. "His name's Brad Perry. I've been seeing him for years." He shrugged. "What can it hurt?"

As he left, Dennis looked at the card. He pulled out his wallet, slid it in and looked at the door. "For years," Dennis quipped. "What can it help?"

Dennis spent the weekend home in his study, alone to work on a new project. Brian bailed him out of the Woodpine deal, but it certainly wasn't going to go that way again. This project, in fact, was threatening to make or break his career.

One creative block after the other triggered the start of panic. He paced the floor. He couldn't concentrate and poured a drink to relax. Suddenly, Shane barged in with Mr. Duffy. "Get out!" Dennis screamed. "I'm trying to get some work done in here."

Mr. Duffy let out a growl and ran out. Tracey grabbed her startled son, shot Dennis a look that could kill, and then closed the door behind them.

"Damn it," Dennis roared and tossed a ream of papers into the air. As they floated to the floor, he walked over to the window. His kids were out playing in the backyard. He tipped the glass to his lips and drank hard. With one last swallow, he slammed down the glass and put on his jacket.

Beneath a shedding tree, Dennis approached Shane. "Sorry about yelling," he said. "Dad's just been tired lately."

Without a hint of resentment, the boy shrugged. "That's okay, Dad. Wanna have a game of catch?"

Dennis smiled, and grabbed two mitts from the shed. Shane squirmed with excitement.

From the moment the ball was thrown, neither could stop smiling.

Dennis punched his fist into an old catcher's mitt, while Shane bit on his tongue in a display of complete concentration. "Come on, Shane," Dennis encouraged. "Right down the pipe. Let's see what you've got."

The boy let one fly. The slap of leather caused Dennis to stand and pump his arm, proudly. "Strike!"

Shane glowed. "Yes!"

"That's what I'm talking about," Dennis said. "You keep throwing the ball like that, little man, and you'll be playing for the Red Sox before you know it."

The two continued to play catch, laughing and sharing the early autumn sunshine. Mr. Duffy was just happy to run back and forth between them. Tracey looked out the window and shook her worried head. One second he was screaming at Shane, and the next he was playing with him.

When they finally came in from their game, Dennis found Tracey and Tyler seated at a cluttered kitchen table. Tracey was helping their youngest boy with a fundamental math problem: 1 plus 4. Tyler struggled just as much with the reasons for learning the math than with the problems themselves.

Without thinking, Dennis took a seat. Then, without meaning to, he took over.

"It's stupid," Tyler claimed. "I can't."

Tracey began to answer. "Tyler, I already told you..."

"It's not stupid, Ty," Dennis interrupted. "And we never use the word *can't* around here." Dennis smiled. "Ty, math is just another way to open your mind and flex your brain." He lifted his arm to flex his bicep. In spite of himself, Tyler giggled. Dennis ruffled the small boy's hair.

Tracey stood. "My God, Dennis. When did we stop working as a team?"

Dennis felt confused. "Huh?"

She shook her head and walked away.

"Five," Tyler answered.

"What?" Dennis asked, looking back at his son.

"The answer is five," said the young boy.

Dennis looked down at the paper. One eyebrow rose in a display of confirmation. "You're absolutely right. Five it is." He looked toward the living room where Tracey had disappeared and shook his head. He hadn't meant to interfere and felt bad.

Tyler patiently awaited his father's attention.

Dennis caught his son's blank face and smiled. "I'm telling you, Ty, all you have to do is apply yourself and someday you'll be flying the space shuttle for NASA."

Tyler's brow considered the possibility. Suddenly, his innocent eyes showed belief.

Dennis and Tyler became consumed in the remaining problems of addition, and completed the homework in record time.

Once his boys had been tended to, Dennis ventured off to his little girl. He knelt beside Beth in a bedroom awash in pink. Together, they spoke to God. Beth prayed, "Now I lay me down to sleep. I pray the Lord my soul to keep. If I should die before I wake. I pray the Lord my soul to take."

There was a pause. Dennis nodded for her to continue.

"Father," she said, "please bless my Mom, my Dad, my brothers and Mr. Duffy- our dog. Amen." As an afterthought, she added, "Oh, and God, please make Mom and Dad stop fighting."

"Amen," Dennis agreed, and tucked his little girl into bed – pulling the covers under her chin. He finished the nightly ritual with a kiss. "Sweet dreams, Princess," he whispered.

"Sweet dreams, Daddy."

He paused at the door to catch one last glimpse of his sleeping angel. Shaking his sad head at her final request, he turned off the light.

In their darkened bedroom, Dennis threw on a pair of pajama bottoms. Tracey wore an old pair of flannels. They slid beneath the bed covers, bitter and exhausted.

"You're going to have to see the kids on the bus tomorrow," Tracey informed him. "I have an early interview. Joe set a ten o'clock deadline."

Dennis couldn't hold back. "That's nice of Joe. Doesn't he remember that you still have kids? I don't understand why he can't give the early assignments to someone else."

Tracey sighed, halting Dennis's spiel. Moonlight illuminated their silhouettes. She rolled over and placed her back to him. With a yawn, she threw in the last dig of the night. "Joe understands that the kids have a father, too."

Dennis chuckled, sarcastically.

"Well, Goodnight," she muttered.

Dennis stretched to give her a kiss.

She buried her head in a pillow.

"What is it now?" he asked.

"Nothing. I'm just not feeling well, that's all. Is that okay?"

"I guess it has to be okay," he snickered. "Doesn't it?"

There was an aggravated pause.

"Seems to me you should go see a doctor," he continued. "You haven't felt well in weeks." There was a pause. "At least not with me."

She exploded. "What does that mean – at least not with you?"

He placed his hands behind his head, and silently stared at the darkness. Tracey pretended to fall asleep. Her pride would prove no match for the unforgiving anxiety that kept him up, though. The night would be spent in worry over Tracey having an affair at work. *Perhaps with that photographer, Pete, whom she's spoken of,* he thought. Dennis's imagination was back in high gear. This time, however, it wasn't about to take him to any place nice.

~ VII ~

Streetlights strobe in and out of the tinted windows. A soft ballad played on the stereo and the windshield wipers kept perfect beat to it all. The children were dressed in Halloween costumes.

Dennis rubbed the back of his neck, trying desperately to work out the knots. Looking to his right, he found Tracey dozing off. He released an agitated breath before his eyes began dotting between the road ahead of him and the rear-view mirror. Shane, Beth and Tyler all slept. Dennis's eyes continued to search behind him and a look of serious concern covered his face. The rain continued to fall.

"Now what's bothering you?" Tracey asked, breaking the thick silence.

Dennis was startled. He exhaled heavy, but his wide eyes never left the rear-view mirror. Tracey turned her head to look behind them. There was nothing there.

"Now what's bothering me?" he roared. "NOW WHAT'S BOTHERING ME? WHAT DO YOU THINK'S BOTHERING ME?" At the conclusion of his outrage, spit covered his mouth.

Tracey gritted her teeth, and prepared to do battle. Some shuffling from the backseat, however, halted her – sending her into a state of frustration. "Who do you think you are?" she hissed, "talking to me like that? I REALLY HAVE HAD IT WITH YOU!"

Dennis glared at her. There was an equal lack of love in his eyes. He continued at a hush. "You've had it with me? What a joke! I bet you haven't had it with Pete, though, have you?"

The two stared at each other with disgust.

"As a matter of fact," he added, "I think your boyfriend is right behind us. Maybe he's going to follow us to the house to do some trick-or-treating?"

Tracey turned to look out the rear window again, but snapped back when she realized her petty husband was mistaken.

"You really are such a child, Dennis," she said. "I told you weeks ago, Pete is my colleague and my friend and if you can't handle that, then too bad."

"TOO BAD?" he screeched.

"Yeah, too bad! If you weren't so busy at work, so preoccupied with everyone but me, then I wouldn't need Pete – or anyone else to confide in." She started to cry. "If you remembered how to be a husband, then…"

Dennis slammed his fist off the steering wheel, causing Tracey to shut up. The kids shifted uneasily in the back seat.

"THAT'S NICE!" she growled. "Keep acting like an animal. The kids don't have enough to be afraid of."

Dennis scanned the rear-view and quieted his tone. "What do the kids have to be afraid of, Trace … having their mother trade in their father for a newspaper photographer?"

"NO," she retorted at a scream, "HAVING THEIR MOTHER FIND A REAL MAN WHO…"

"NO MORE. PLEASE!" Beth begged. "I can't take it anymore." And the contagious weeping began.

Tracey leaned over the front seat to find each of her children frightened and sobbing. Dennis caught the same in the rear-view. Tracey turned back slightly and took the last shot. "See what your insane jealousies have done to this family? It's going to end, Dennis. I swear it. You'll be living alone before I allow these kids to live in fear another day."

Dennis cracked the window to allow in a blast of fresh air. The anger had his face so red, it felt ready to burst. Tracey was blaming the family problems on him, and not the affair she was obviously trying to keep secret.

While she shook with rage, Tracey comforted her children. Dennis had no right to accuse her of something she'd never do. It was his fault that they'd grown apart, not hers. And if anyone was cheating, it was he.

Sobs and sniffles played nicely with the rain on the windows. The entire family returned home in despair.

Once the children were put to bed, Tracey took her shower. Dennis stepped into the children's rooms to say his goodnights. From the boys' room to Beth's bedroom, he shouldered the brunt of their fears.

"Dad?" Shane asked.

"What is it, buddy?"

"Are you and Mom gonna split up?"

Dennis took a seat on the bottom bunk. "I want you guys to know that Mom and I owe you kids an apology. We shouldn't be fighting in front of you. It's wrong, and I'm sorry."

There was a pause. The boys still awaited an answer.

Dennis spoke softly. "I don't want you guys worrying about anybody splitting up. Mom and I are dealing with some adult issues – things that you guys shouldn't be concerned with."

"But are you gonna be livin' alone like Ma said?" Tyler asked.

"No, son. I'm not going anywhere and neither is Mom." In response to their doubtful eyes, Dennis concluded, "You have my word."

Both boys snuggled beneath their covers, satisfied with their father's solemn promise. Smiles replaced anxious frowns. He kissed them both and headed to Beth's room.

The little girl was sitting up, waiting for her Dad. Tearfully, she began, "Daddy, I was wonderin'…"

Dennis hurried to her bed and placed his finger to her tiny, trembling lips. "Don't wonder about anything, Princess. Just because Mom and I fight, that doesn't mean that anything's going to change around here, okay?"

He kissed her cheek and ran his fingers through her hair. "I love you and your brothers more than you could ever imagine. Mom and I just have to find a way to stop fighting." He kissed her. "For now, just know that Mom and I love each other. Now get some sleep."

He left his daughter in a much happier state than when he'd found her.

Walking into the master bedroom, Dennis discovered Tracey in bed. She pretended to be sleeping.

"Trace?" he whispered.

There was silence. He placed his hand on her shoulder.

"Don't you dare touch me," she hissed.

He didn't expect the hatred in her voice and it startled him.

"And I wasn't kidding," she said. "If you can't control your adolescent paranoia, then maybe you should start looking for another place to live."

He grabbed for her, but she violently shook off his attempt at tenderness.

"Come on now, Trace," he pleaded. "You're being ridiculous. I know we've been through a rough stretch, but…"

With murder in her eyes, Tracey turned to face him. She grabbed his pillow and threw it in his face. "Get away from me," she hissed. "I don't want you near me."

"But Hon, the kids."

She only spoke with more conviction. "GET OUT OF MY BED!"

Dennis sat at the edge of the bed with his mouth hung open. Physically, he and Tracey were only a few feet apart. In actuality, they were worlds removed from each other. Reality was frightening. He feared most that he'd made a grave mistake by not letting her steal a peek into his personal little hell.

Just as Tracey saw the kids onto the bus, Pete Loban pulled up in his van. She forced a smile. The photographer was late, juggling a camera bag with two steaming coffees. His happy face changed when he realized something was wrong.

"Don't you look like crap," he teased. "Didn't want to take off the Halloween mask just yet, huh?"

She smirked. "Thanks. I really needed one of your compliments this morning." With a wave of her hand, she beckoned him. "Come on in. I just need to shut off the iron."

Pete handed her a coffee and followed her in. In the kitchen, he took notice of the wall clock and looked at his watch. Placing the timepiece to his ear, he shook his head. While Tracey unplugged the iron, he removed the watch and winded it. He looked at Tracey. She was trembling. "Hey, what's up? More trouble in paradise?"

She shrugged, and opened her mouth to speak when the tears started to flow. Pete placed his watch on the kitchen counter and approached her. He put his arm around her and led her to the door. "Come on, Trace. You can tell me on the way."

Tracey fumbled with her pocketbook and a handful of notepads. Suddenly, she remembered the interview and felt desperate. Pete picked up on it. "And the world won't stop turning if we're late either," he assured her with a smile. "Well, maybe not Joe's world, but Joe's world is due for a break anyway."

Tracey grinned and stepped into the photographer's van. Pete started it, turned off the radio and drove away from the curb right past Dennis's hidden Lexus.

As they rolled by, Dennis struggled for air. His knuckles, now white, were wrapped around the steering wheel – which threatened to crack under the pressure. He tried to scream, but only a squeak would escape. He'd been betrayed and his heart ached with a pain he'd never known.

A mile away, Tracey turned to Pete. "I'm so sorry to put this on you," she said.

Pete placed his hand on hers. "Now you're insulting me. I thought we were friends."

She nodded. After grabbing a tissue from her purse, she began to ramble. "I just don't know anymore, Pete. Things haven't been great with Dennis for months, but now it's gotten so that it's unbearable. He yells at me in front of the kids. When I think something is bothering him and I ask what it is, he snaps at me. He won't tell me anything. He constantly accuses me of cheating."

"Cheating?"

Tracey grinned through the sniffles. "Yeah. And of all people...with you."

In spite of the heavy situation, Pete released a hearty chuckle. "No offense, but did you tell him that you're not my type?"

"No, I didn't. Your sexual preference is none of his business. It doesn't matter, anyway. I've never given him any reason to mistrust me. Instead, I gave up my career to raise our kids. Now that I'm getting some of it back…"

"I don't get it," Pete said. "When did all of this start?"

"Right when Tyler started first grade and I decided to go back to work. I haven't been able to communicate with him since. Everything turns into a fight."

"If you ask me, Trace, you guys need to get into counseling. At the very least, you could both learn not to fight in front of those beautiful kids."

Tracey nodded. "I suggested it, months back, but he said that things would get better; that he was just going through a tough time and I should understand – be more patient." She became more upset. "I really think there's something more – something he's not telling me. Something's very wrong. He's been so different. Maybe he's the one who's been playing around?"

"Easy with the accusations, Gumshoe," Pete joked. "You know how that feels. If you ask me, you guys just need to reopen the love lines. You know – a little wine, a little sweet talk, and then…" Pete made some vulgar suggestions, making Tracey slap his arm in fun.

"Stop it, you goof. This is serious."

"I'm just teasing." He laughed. "And I know it's serious. But maybe that's half the problem. If you and Dennis didn't take everything so serious, then maybe life would be happier?"

The van pulled out in front of City Hall where the interview was scheduled. Pete checked the time. "Shoot, I forgot my watch at your house. What time you got?"

She checked her wristwatch and smiled. "We're just in time."

Regaining her composure, she applied her makeup while Pete parked. With a nod, she opened the door and got out. "I can't thank you enough," she said. "I feel better already. I only wish Dennis knew how innocent our friendship is; how much I miss being able to talk to him like this."

Pete winked. "I don't suppose he ever will unless you tell him."

"You're probably right," she said. "I'll try talking to him again tonight." Her eyes filled with tears again. "I've really missed him, Pete."

Pete grinned and raised an eyebrow. Tracey buttoned her coat, looked back at her partner and then put on her game face. Pete's smile widened.

~ VIII ~

It was late morning before Dennis found himself sitting alone in the New Dimensions parking lot. His shoulders drooped from the weight of losing his unfaithful wife. Heavy bags hung under his eyes from a full week's loss of sleep. The cars surrounding him were deserted. With the exception of his heavy sobbing, it was silent.

Jim Hancock pulled up alongside him. He got out of his car and approached. Dennis wiped his eyes, took a deep breath and rolled down the window.

"So this is where you find your inspiration?" Jim kidded.

Dennis looked up, but the lump in his throat would not allow him to speak.

Jim decided to cut to the chase. His tone turned serious. "What's the status on Brighams's Auto World?"

Dennis looked at his boss with torment in his eyes. There was alcohol on his breath and Jim could smell it. Furthermore, he spotted a flask of brandy sitting on the passenger side floor. The bottle was half-empty. Jim shook his head. "You go see a doctor yet?" he asked.

"Yeah, I did," Dennis mumbled. "He said everything looks fine. My cholesterol is a little high, but everything else…"

"That's not the type of doctor I'm talking about."

Dennis pondered the insinuation. "Jim, please!" he barked. "I don't need you telling me how to conduct my personal business."

"Yeah Dennis, you do need me telling you how to conduct your personal business. You've been to work three times in the last two weeks. When you do show, you're either drunk, or you pawn off your work to one of our junior people."

Dennis looked surprised.

Jim shook his head. "You don't think I've been in the business long enough to recognize the difference between a rookie's work and that of a seasoned veteran?"

Dennis never answered. He couldn't have cared less. His mind was on Tracey.

"We were lucky to save the account," Jim said. "But it's unacceptable, Dennis."

Dennis never batted an eye. Jim shook his head again. As if searching for strength, he looked up at the sky and bent again to drop the hammer. "Dennis, I was going to talk to you this morning anyway. So, I guess this place is as good as anywhere." They locked eyes. Jim let it fly. "I've been in touch with benefits. The company's prepared to assist you in anyway possible; therapy, rehab, whatever you need, but for the time being consider yourself..."

"Fired?"

"On vacation, Dennis. Consider yourself on vacation until you pull yourself together."

Dennis started up the Lexus and threw it into reverse. Squealing the tires out of his executive parking spot, he just missed Jim's feet – leaving his boss standing in the lot, cursing his name. Dennis slammed the steering wheel. "What else can I possibly lose?"

In what seemed like seconds, Dennis sped into his driveway, jumped out of the car and slammed the door.

As he proceeded through the kitchen to grab a beer, he stopped. There was an unfamiliar wristwatch sitting on the counter. He picked it up and turned it over. It read: *To Pete. With Love, Pat.*

He let out a shriek and threw the watch on the floor where it broke into a hundred pieces. In a fit of blinding rage, he began smashing everything he could get his hands on.

At the end of the violent outburst, he collapsed to the floor where he wept, mournfully. With his head in both hands, he screamed, "HOW COULD SHE DO THIS TO ME? WHY TRACEY? WHY?" His cries quickly turned to whimpers.

Tracey picked up the phone and dialed New Dimensions Advertising. Dennis's secretary answered.

"Hi Sue. Can I speak with Dennis, please."

There was an awkward moment of silence. Sue cleared her throat. "I'm sorry, Mrs. Anderson... Mr. Anderson didn't tell you?"

"Tell me what?"

There was a long pause. "That he's on a leave of absence."

Tracey's jaw touched her chest. "I'm sorry. Did you just say that he's taken a leave of absence?"

"No. Not exactly," Sue explained. "Mr. Anderson didn't have a choice."

Tracey nearly dropped the phone. "Well now, isn't that just wonderful."

She hung up and called home. The answering machine picked up and the kids greeted her in chorus. "Hi! You've reached the Andersons. Please leave a message and we'll get right back to ya. Have a great day!"

"Unbelievable," she hissed, long before the machine beeped to receive the message.

When she returned home with the kids, she couldn't have been more furious. And then she walked into the kitchen.

While her wide eyes surveyed the damage, shock stopped her dead in her tracks. "Go to your rooms," she ordered the children, and then stormed into the living room. Dennis was sitting in his recliner, drunk.

"What did you do to my kitchen?" she yelled.

"How long has it been going on?" Dennis asked in a hoarse whisper.

"What? I just asked you a question and I want an answer."

Dennis leapt to his feet. There was madness in his eyes. "AND I JUST ASKED YOU HOW LONG YOU'VE BEEN CHEATING ON ME?"

Tracey's emotions seesawed between rage and fear. She eventually returned the scream. "GET OUT. GET OUT NOW!"

He grabbed her arm, pulled her to him and stuffed the broken watch in her face. Her rage was instantly consumed by fear.

He screamed even louder. "RIGHT IN OUR OWN HOME?"

"Stop it, Dennis, you're hurting me," she cried. "Let go of my arm." The tears began to pour.

He let go and threw the watch at the TV, causing the screen to crack. "I swear to God," he slurred. "I'll kill somebody before this family is taken from me."

He walked to the fireplace, grabbed a framed photo of the family from the cluttered mantle and threw it against the wall where it shattered into pieces.

Tracey took the opportunity to run into the master bedroom. Hyperventilating, she locked the door behind her and picked up the phone. She punched in the numbers 911. Just then, something else smashed against the wall in the living room.

"What is the nature of your emergency?" the monotone voice inquired.

"My husband's tearing our house apart. And he's threatened to kill…Oh God…my kids are upstairs…Oh, dear God."

"Ma'am, you need to calm down and tell me the address."

"It's 19 Thornton Street…in…in…Westport. Please hurry. I've never seen him like this!" By now she was panting. "Oh, God…my kids are listening to this upstairs."

Lightheaded and trembling, Dennis stood outside the door and banged away. "OPEN THIS DAMN DOOR, TRACEY. WE'RE NOT DONE TALKING!"

With one hand on the knob, Tracey stood on the other side of the door. She started for the lock when he pounded his fist wildly against the wood. "OPEN THIS DOOR BEFORE I BREAK IT DOWN," he screeched.

Panicked, she warned, "Dennis, I just called the cops and they're on the way. Please stop. Please think of the kids and stop this insanity."

For the first time, Dennis thought about his children listening upstairs. He turned, threw his back against the door and collapsed to the floor. Placing his face into his trembling hands, he began crying uncontrollably. "I lost my job today, Trace," he babbled in a drunken daze. "And then I lost my wife." He began to hyperventilate. "OH…GOD…please dear God…not…my…kids…too."

Tracey cried along with him, but for different reasons.

There was a loud knock at the front door before a deep voice called out. "OPEN UP, IT'S THE POLICE."

One police officer absorbed the damage of the violent outburst, while his partner stood between Dennis and a visibly shaken Tracey. The kids peeked through the banisters of the staircase that led upstairs. Each was trembling and sobbed to each twitch. They listened to the brief interview.

"Ma'am, can you tell me what happened here?" the first police officer inquired.

Dennis tried to answer. "Officer, I…"

The cop was quick. "I WASN'T TALKING TO YOU, PAL. YOU'LL SPEAK WHEN I ASK YOU TO." He looked back at Tracey. "Go ahead, Ma'am."

Tracey's voice was shaky. "When I came home, the kitchen was already destroyed. I sent the kids upstairs and asked my husband what happened. He started ranting and raving about me cheating on him with another man." The sobbing began.

Through his staggering drunkenness, Dennis tried again. "Officer, please, it's just a misunderstanding between my wife and I."

"YOU OPEN YOUR MOUTH AGAIN AND I'LL SLAP THE CUFFS ON YOU," the cop roared. "UNDERSTAND?"

Dennis quickly sobered up. Tracey wouldn't even look at him, but struggled to go on. "He grabbed me by the arm, showed me a broken watch and threw it at the TV. He started smashing things and making threats." She couldn't finish.

The second police officer grabbed his portable radio and pushed the button. There was one squelch before he spoke. "Central, be advised, we'll be transporting one on Domestic Assault charges."

The man's younger partner removed a set of handcuffs from his belt and grabbed Dennis by the arm.

Dennis panicked. "Trace, PLEASE!" he squealed. "Tell them this is a mistake."

Tracey shared his anxiety. "Sir, please," she pleaded. "Not here.

Not in front of our children."

Dennis scowled at her once before pulling away from the officer. The second cop, however, wouldn't have any of it. Like a jungle cat, he pounced on Dennis and wrestled him to the floor. Of all times, Shane ran to the scene. "Stop hurting my Dad!" he screamed. "Mom, make them stop!"

Tracey could only babble. "PLEASE...Oh, God...not here."

Dennis was placed face down. As the first police officer knelt on his back, the other forced Dennis's arms behind his back. Dennis bucked and convulsed, groaning like a wounded animal.

"This is my home," he panted through gritted teeth. He finally surrendered to the officers' manhandling, and his tense body went limp. "Come on," he whimpered. "Not in front of my kids."

Beth and Tyler followed their brother out and huddled around Tracey, latching onto her as if they were watching their father's slaughter. Everyone was crying. Handcuffs were applied and Dennis was jerked to his feet.

"I'm sorry, Ma'am," the older officer claimed. "Under these circumstances, we have no choice but to arrest."

Tracey was in shock. "But I...I...I."

Dennis winced from the pain in his wrists. Each officer grabbed an arm and began walking him out of the house. He was looking at Tracey with contempt and hatred when he caught the horror in his children's eyes. Everyone froze. To his surprise, the officers allowed him a moment to speak. He could barely get the words out. They were stuck behind the lump in his throat. "Guys, I'm so sorry you had to see this. But don't you worry about Dad, okay? It's all just a big mistake. Mom and I will clear the whole thing up."

The kids ran to him and wrapped their arms around his quivering legs. Three sets of eyes looked up and searched for their father's comfort.

"I love you guys more than anything in the world," he vowed, "always remember that." He fought back the tears. "And I'll be home soon. I promise."

As the officers escorted him out of the house, Tracey dropped to her knees and embraced her frightened children. Shane, however, refused his mother's comfort. They grieved, violently. Between sobs, the echo of a deep voice traveled back into the house. "You have the right to remain silent, tough guy. You have the right to an attorney." The rest drifted off with any hopes of sleep.

Dennis's fingers were stained black. His belt and shoes had already been removed from him when he threw a quarter into the pay phone and dialed home. The kids sounded happy. "Hi! You've reached the Andersons. Please leave a message and we'll get right back to ya. Have a great day!"

His eyes filled with tears. The booking officers took notice. A young police officer grabbed him by the arm and chuckled. "Well Pal," he said, "that's your one phone call. Looks like you'll be spending the night at the roach motel."

The older officer understood more compassion. He pulled his inexperienced partner's arm off Dennis, reached into his pocket and threw their prisoner a quarter. Dennis was shocked.

"Oh, thanks anyway," Dennis mumbled, "but I have no one else to call." He handed back the coin.

The officer looked confused. "What about your attorney? Don't you want to make bail and get out of here?"

Dennis shook his head. "I don't want to bother him at home. I'll call him in the morning." He shrugged. "If it's just the same, I'll stay here?"

The older officer offered a solemn nod and escorted his pathetic prisoner into one of the dingy cells. Dennis took a seat on the bunk. Within seconds, he was rolled into the fetal position where a whole new feeling tapped him on the shoulder.

There was an evil force that pulled at him and though he didn't want to go, his tired mind gave in. The tunnel of depression was dark and he saw no end. Carrying a tremendous weight upon his shoulders, he only wished to rest, perhaps sleep forever, but the fear of staying in this tunnel of hell made him forge ahead. He sensed there were others in the tunnel, but a vicious loneliness tore at his soul. Each step was agonizing, as he went nowhere. Finally collapsing onto a cold floor, he wondered if anyone even knew that he was lost; if anyone even knew how to pull him out. While one last tear tumbled down his twisted face, a tormenting fear welled up inside of him. He'd reached despair, perhaps, for him – the end.

Life at the Anderson Home was no happier. Beth and Tyler went to bed, but Shane wouldn't hear of it. He sat on the stairs, eavesdropping on his Mom's telephone conversation.

As she cleaned the kitchen, Tracey rested the phone between her ear and shoulder. She was an emotional wreck. "You had to see him, Jenn. He was a madman. I really didn't know if he was going to hurt me."

"That son-of-a—," Jenn squawked, "putting his hands on you like that right in front of the kids. You're going to press charges, right?"

Tracey wept sorrowfully. "The police told me that it's out of my hands. They said they're charging Dennis with Domestic Assault."

Shane stormed up to his room.

"Good enough," Jenn said.

Tracey shook her head. "I know Jenn, but it's just…"

"IT'S JUST NOTHING! The kids don't need to see that stuff, Trace. And you certainly don't need to live like that either. No woman does."

"I know. I know," Tracey admitted. "I didn't think it would come to this, but I realize now that Dennis really does need professional help."

"And he'll get it," Jenn snickered, "right where he belongs."

~ IX ~

Handcuffed, Dennis was escorted into the court for his arraignment. Tracey gasped at the sight of it. His eyes quickly found her. He felt numb. She couldn't read his feelings. The Assistant District Attorney stood before her, breaking their eye contact. "Mrs. Anderson," he said, "even though the state is charging you're husband, we're going to require that you testify."

Tracey felt sick. Before she could respond, though, the attorney added, "And unfortunately, the only way we can guarantee your family's safety is for you to request a restraining order."

Tracey shook her head no. Tears rolled down her cheeks.

"I've seen hundreds of these cases, Mrs. Anderson," the A.D.A. claimed, "and many end up..." He stopped and searched her face. "Why don't we just impose a temporary order then – until your husband gets help for his anger?"

Hesitantly, Tracey nodded. As the A.D.A. smiled, the judge entered. Everyone rose. The charges were read: *One count, Domestic Assault. One count, resisting arrest.*

"Mr. Anderson, how do you plead to the charge of assault and battery?" the judge asked.

Charles Robertson, the family attorney, clasped his hands together. "Not guilty, Your Honor."

The Assistant District Attorney winked at Tracey, and then turned to give his spiel. She never felt more ill. "Your Honor," he said, "Mrs. Anderson is requesting an immediate 209A, restraining order. Due to the circumstances, I believe this would be most prudent at this time."

Tracey recoiled at the request. The judge's hand motioned to begin the proceedings.

The A.D.A. recited the details of the horrible night's events. Both arresting officers testified to the condition of the Anderson's kitchen, the angry state Dennis was in and the bruises that began

69

forming on Tracey Anderson's arm. As if he'd already made his judgment, the judge glared down at Dennis.

Dennis felt removed from the scene – until Tracey was called to the stand. Hesitantly, she stepped up. After being sworn in, the A.D.A. began his line of questioning. "Mrs. Anderson, on the evening in question, did your husband physically damage property within your home?"

Tracey nodded.

"Did he make threats of inflicting bodily harm upon another?"

"Umm…yes he did," she replied, painfully.

The A.D.A. quickened his pace. "Did he also place his hands upon you, causing bruises?"

Tracey felt like she might actually vomit. "Yes," she answered, "but…"

"A yes or no answer will suffice, Mrs. Anderson." The A.D.A. was clearly not a compassionate man.

"No, it won't!" Tracey screeched. Dennis was being painted a monster. Tracey turned to the judge. "Your Honor," she pleaded, "this is my family's future that we're talking about here. I believe I should have the right to speak freely."

The judge looked over at Dennis, and then back at Tracey. He nodded.

"My husband did do everything that you've said, but he was drunk." She shook her head. "I know that alcohol isn't a defense, or even an excuse for his actions, but Dennis has never been a violent man. He's always been a good husband and a wonderful father." She paused to breathe. "Things have gotten out of hand lately and he's shown signs of violence, but until last night he never physically acted on them. I suppose everything came to a head yesterday. Dennis lost his job…"

The judge shifted uneasily at the discovery of Dennis's recent unemployment.

Tracey struggled to finish. "He came home and found a male watch belonging to a colleague of mine. Even though I've been true to him, he believes I've been unfaithful." The tears started. "All I'm saying is...my husband is not a criminal. He's a man that cannot contain his temper. He's a man who needs help." The sobbing became worse. "I've...I've...tried to be there for him." She looked at the judge. "I'm begging you, please get him help."

The judge straightened himself before he spoke. "Mrs. Anderson. I appreciate your candidness. However, in all good conscience, this court must consider the welfare of your children above all else. So I must ask you now, after yesterday's ordeal, do you believe that your children will be completely safe in the presence of their father?"

Tracey looked at Dennis and the tears flowed faster. Dennis leaned forward. As he awaited his real sentence, panic rushed through his veins.

"No, not until Dennis gets help for his anger." She trembled at the truth of it. "No, I don't think that our children are completely safe around him."

Attorney Robertson leapt to his feet. "Your Honor, I object! I haven't even had the opportunity to defend Mr. Anderson." He was talking so fast that he began to stutter. "We haven't come to a finding on the charges. How can we even entertain the notion of a restraining order?"

The judge peered down his rigid nose. "Mr. Robertson, let me be frank. This is my court and I have been granted great discretion in my rulings on family matters. So let me fill you in: Your client has no past criminal record and until yesterday, he was gainfully employed. Therefore, this court does not view him as someone who needs to serve jail time. However, it is quite evident that something is going on with Mr. Anderson that is not in the best interest of his small children." Scanning over the piece of paper before him, his stern eyes returned to the shocked lawyer. "This court will impose a temporary 209A on behalf of Mrs. Anderson and her children. However, as there is no prior record, I am willing to dispose of the case this morning. If your client is so willing, I'd be willing to impose a three-year pre-trial sentence of probation."

"But, Your Honor," was all Attorney Robertson had left.

"There are no buts here, Mr. Robertson," the snarling judge

advised. He pointed at Dennis. "Mr. Anderson, shame on you for putting your children through such trauma. You need to find yourself some help, Sir."

"Please, Your Honor," Dennis whimpered. "Please don't take my kids from me."

When the judge broke eye contact, Dennis knew that his plea had fallen upon deaf ears. The court felt it was working in the best interest of the children. Sharp pains threatened to bend Dennis in half.

Attorney Robertson addressed the court. "May I have a moment with my client, your Honor?"

"Granted," the judge said.

Robertson pulled Dennis aside. There was urgency in his movements and tone. "Dennis, listen to me now. Based on what I've heard here today, this is the best deal we'll get."

Dennis panicked. "The best? What about my kids?"

"Pre-trial probation has nothing to do with the 209A," Robertson said.

"Chuck, please!" Dennis's body trembled near the brink of convulsion.

"Dennis, you need to accept it," Robertson advised. "You're not going to see the kids for awhile. The judge will impose the restraining order." He patted Dennis's shoulder. "But as long as you comply with the terms of the probation, after three years, the case will get dismissed."

As if the man missed the real punishment, Dennis glared at his attorney. "Fine," he muttered in despair.

Robertson addressed the court once again. "Your Honor, my client is willing to accept your recommendation on the assault and battery charge."

The judge nodded and noted this on his documentation. Seconds later, he looked back at Dennis. "Mr. Anderson, I'm sorry, but…"

To Dennis, the rest sounded like *blah…blah…blah…* He

collapsed back into his chair. To him, being restrained from seeing his children was equivalent to receiving the death sentence. The remainder of the hearing passed as some cruel haze. In the end, he was found guilty of Domestic Assault. Probation was imposed for a period of three years, along with a mandate to attend Domestic Violence classes for a period of two months. Upon graduating from the program, visitation with his children would be further entertained by the court.

The judge left the bench long before Dennis emerged from his fog. In fact, it took a few nudges from Attorney Robertson to bring him back. "Dennis, are you even listening to me?" Robertson asked.

"What? What's that Chuck?" Everything was so blurry.

"There was nothing more I could do," the sad lawyer admitted. "These proceedings are a crapshoot, and today we drew the wrong judge. He's a tough one. He doesn't play around when it comes to Domestic Violence."

Dennis remained catatonic. Robertson grabbed his arm. "Listen to me, Dennis! The judge has imposed some stiff sanctions here. We have a court date scheduled in two months. I know it hurts, but in the meantime, you have to stay clear of Tracey and the kids. The restraining order is only temporary, but it's still no contact." He finally slowed down. "It's also imperative that you attend every Domestic Abuse class. And I promise you, Dennis: If you violate the restraining order, this judge will revoke your probation and send you right to jail. Understand?"

Dennis shrugged. "I don't understand anything anymore, Chuck."

Reality was that he couldn't see his children for two unbearable months. The rest just didn't matter. In a room full of people, he felt so alone. On her way out of the courtroom, Tracey wiped her eyes and hesitated before her broken husband. He couldn't even look at her. His despair wouldn't allow it.

It was late when Dennis picked up the motel room's phone. He'd spent hours going through every detail in his tired mind, and all the blame circled straight back to Tracey. At the risk of violating the restraining order and going to jail, he called her.

"Hello?" Tracey sounded exhausted.

"You have no right to take my kids from me," he screamed.

"I have every right, Dennis," she answered, calmly. "A big part of my job as a Mom is to protect them."

"From me? Protect them from me?"

"Look Dennis, you left me no choice – acting like an animal, destroying the house…making those threats. The kids shouldn't have to live like that."

"Tracey, PLEASE!" he cried. "I love the kids. I would never hurt them. You know that."

"But I don't know that, Dennis," she whimpered. "I don't know anything about you anymore. You're angry, and you're violent." There was a terrible pause. "Look, God only knows what's going to happen to our marriage, but as far as the kids, I don't want to keep them from you. They need you." She grew strong again. "But until you get help, I don't feel comfortable with you around them."

He couldn't hold back any longer. "YOU BETRAYED ME! I NEEDED YOU, AND YOU BETRAYED ME. SO LET'S FORGET ABOUT THE MARRIAGE, OKAY? AS FAR AS THE KIDS, I'M THEIR FATHER. I HELPED BRING THEM INTO THE WORLD."

"Dennis," she interrupted. "I'm not going to be victimized by your malicious outbursts anymore. Go get help, and then we'll talk. If you call here again, I'll call the police." Although she was confident in her decisions, she'd never felt so low.

Dennis slammed down the phone. Tracey was dead wrong. The kids were the furthest from risk while in his presence. He grabbed a whiskey bottle and tipped it to the ceiling. He'd hit bottom. In one day, he'd lost everything that meant anything to him.

An entire world away, Tracey sat on the phone with her sister. As usual, Shane sat on the stairs and listened in. Tracey was a babbling fool. "But you don't understand, Jenn. He lost his job. He found Pete's watch on the kitchen counter. He needed me to be there for him. He needed me."

"Whoa, Trace," Jenn said. "I understand the whole marriage thing, but how were you supposed to be there for him…as a punching bag?"

"It wasn't like that," Tracey swore. "He was drunk."

"Yeah. And he's been drunk for months. The judge was right to issue the restraining order."

"My family's destroyed, Jenn. Do you understand that?" Tracey was coming apart at the seams. "The kids can't sleep. They constantly ask for their father. What do I tell them? Huh, Jenn?"

"Tell them the truth. Tell them that their father couldn't keep his hands to himself."

Just then, Shane walked in and looked up at Tracey. "You don't have to tell us anything," he screamed. "We know." Tears covered his face. "We know that you made Dad go away and now you won't let him come back. We know!"

Tracey was mortified. "Jenn, I'll talk to you later," she muttered and hung up. She dropped to her knees and opened her arms to embrace her eldest son. "Shane, Mommy didn't…"

Shane avoided her touch and headed to his room where he could mourn with his siblings.

The grief had Tracey bent in half. "My God," she cried. "What have we done?"

It didn't take long for Dennis to become staggering drunk. And, it took even less time for the patrons at Bobby's Lounge to stay clear of him. When Bobby shut him off, though, everything came to a head. "Shut off?" Dennis screamed. "Are you nuts?"

"Look, Buddy," Bobby growled, "you've had enough for the both of us, so why don't you just go home."

"Because I don't have a home," Dennis screamed. "That's why!"

The rest came out as one long slur. "I don't have a wife anymore. I don't have kids anymore." His tearing eyes forced Bobby to look away.

Bobby rounded the bar and tried to help Dennis to the door. In return, Dennis stood and threw a punch that missed the bartender by a mile – landing him on his rear end.

"Any other day," Bobby warned, "and you'd be wearing my boot in your backside. But it's pretty clear to me that no one's gonna do anything to you that you haven't already done to yourself."

Bobby extended his hand. Dennis eventually took it and slid on to a nearby chair. "I lost everything today," he babbled, "my whole world."

Bobby stepped behind the bar, picked up the phone and called for a taxi. Suddenly, the sound of broken glass grabbed his attention. He rushed back and found Dennis lying on the floor, a broken beer bottle resting in his hand. Blood oozed everywhere. Bobby screamed back to the bar, "Call 911. He's slashed his wrists." Bobby bent to survey the damage and screamed louder. "Hurry! He's bleedin' to death."

~ X ~

Tracey finished an article in the newsroom. Her computer read December 21, 1995. The office was decorated in red and green, with garland hanging everywhere. Pete Loban pulled up a seat at her desk, and threw her a package of snack cakes. "Here. Merry Christmas."

"Oh, you shouldn't have." She giggled. "You're much too kind."

Pete giggled along with her. "It's the least I could do."

Tracey didn't counter. She felt troubled. Pete picked up on it. "So, how's life on the home front?" he asked.

She shrugged. "The same. It's been a little bit easier since my mother moved in, but you know…" The tears were already fighting to break free. "The kids are just devastated, Pete. Shane blames me. Beth and Tyler don't understand why Daddy doesn't come home." She shook her head. "And I'm supposed to play Santa in four days."

"So what do you tell them about Daddy?"

"What can I tell them? I don't even understand what happened myself. It seemed like one minute life was good and the next Dennis was trying to kill himself."

"And how is Dennis, anyway?"

"Not good." The tears finally broke free and gravity took over. "He left the hospital just as soon as they let him. Imagine that? He was minutes away from taking his life, but once they stitched him up, they couldn't even make him stay." She searched for a tissue from her purse. "He refuses to talk to anyone. He thinks I'm trying to destroy him by keeping the kids from him." She looked up at her friend. "But honestly, Pete, I would never…"

Pete grabbed her arm. "Trace, you're doing the right thing. You really are. It's obvious that something pretty dark is going on in Dennis's head." He bent to stare her straight in the eyes. "And until he decides to deal with it, you don't need the kids seeing things that kids don't need to see. Besides, it's in the hands of the court now."

"But what about him? He's still my husband, Pete, and he's so alone right now. He's not working. He won't talk to any of our family or friends. He hasn't even gone to counseling." She reached for another tissue. "We go to court tomorrow on the temporary restraining order. From what I understand, he hasn't attended one of the classes that the judge mandated. Between that and the suicide attempt, the court will never allow him to see the kids. He's spiraling downward, Pete, and I don't know what else I can do for him." She became hysterical and couldn't finish.

Pete stood and rubbed her back. "It's not up to you anymore, Trace. Just take care of your kids and we'll all pray that Dennis finds the strength to get help." He shrugged. "The rest is up to Dennis and the judge."

Unshaven and dirty, Dennis sat with Attorney Robertson; a man who looked equally disgusted to be in court. Tracey entered and made a beeline to her husband.

"Dennis, please," she pleaded. "We need to talk before things get out of control."

Dennis turned to his lawyer. "Chuck, would you please ask her to leave. I don't need to go to jail for violating her restraining order." His heart walked the sharp picket fence between love and hatred.

"Dennis, I didn't want this," she cried.

A court officer approached Tracey and asked that she be seated. The judge entered. Tracey did as she was told – just in time for the nightmare to unfold.

The judge opened a folder, fingered through several reports and looked disapprovingly at Dennis. Ronald Driscoll, Tracey's attorney, broke the silence. "Your Honor, Mr. Anderson has failed to complete the Domestic Abuse program mandated by this court and has also…"

"Take a seat, counselor," the judge barked. "I can read."

The judge turned to Dennis and waved his finger for the defendant to rise. Dennis stood.

"Mr. Anderson," the judge said, "two months ago, when you appeared before me, was I unclear with my instructions?"

"Pardon me, Your Honor?" Dennis's voice was no more than a

squeak.

"Do not try my patience, Mr. Anderson!" the judge roared. Reclaiming his composure, he quieted his tone. "I'll ask again. Did I not instruct you to attend Domestic Abuse Counseling for your explosive temper?"

Dennis nodded. "You did, Your Honor, but I've been sick and…"

"And have not been truly concerned with seeing your children?" the judge finished, sarcastically.

"No, Your Honor, not at all. If you'd allow me to explain."

The judge wouldn't hear it. "I think I've just about had it with your explanations, Mr. Anderson. Why don't you take a seat, get comfortable and allow me to explain a few things to you."

As if he were pushed, Dennis sat. The judge fingered through a folder, wrote down something and cleared his throat. "Mr. Anderson, you were ordered by this court to attend Domestic Abuse counseling. Attorney Driscoll was kind enough to point out that you did not complete the program. However, even he has missed the fact that you did not attend so much as once! I can only perceive this as a blatant act of defiance on your part."

Dennis sat paralyzed. He had tried. No one could ever know that his every waking moment was spent in a tornado of anxiety and depression. He had tried to attend the classes – even made it to the front steps a few times – but the panic had always been too cruel to allow him entrance.

Everyone shifted in his or her seats. Robertson drummed up the courage to speak. "Your Honor, if I may speak on behalf of my client."

"Take a seat, counselor, or find yourself in contempt," the judge bellowed. "Which is it?"

Robertson sat. He noticed Dennis's trembling hands and threw his pencil in a show of frustration. There was nothing more he could do for the broken man.

The judge directed his next words at Dennis. "My records also indicate that since the last time we spoke, Bradley Hospital treated you for wounds consistent with an attempted suicide. Did you attempt to take your life by slashing both your wrists, Mr. Anderson?"

Dennis never flinched. His spirit was all but dead.

The judge was hardly concerned with a response. He went on. "Although Mrs. Anderson has never contacted the authorities, I'd say that it's also a safe bet that you've violated the restraining order, so let me cut to the chase."

Everyone in the courtroom took a deep breath.

"Mr. Anderson, for the time being, your probation will remain intact and you will be spared incarceration. The temporary restraining order protecting your wife and children, however, will be extended to a period of one year."

There was a sudden wave of chaos. The judge raised his voice. "Or until you can convincingly prove to this court that you are not a threat to yourself or anyone around you."

The judge looked right into Dennis's swollen eyes. "Am I clear this time, Mr. Anderson?"

Dennis stood. "A year?" he screamed. "I'd never hurt my kids. They're everything to me. How could you…" The room was closing in around him.

Attorney Robertson grabbed Dennis and forcefully placed him in his seat, preventing a certain jail term. Dennis had a full-blown panic attack for all to see. Tracey could do nothing but sit back and mourn. It was exactly as she feared. Pain had gained momentum and was now completely in control.

Once the room quieted, the judge dropped his cruel demeanor. "Mr. Anderson, contrary to your beliefs right now, I am not an unreasonable man," he explained. "You need professional help. It's also clear to me that this is something you must choose to accept in order for your family to be reunited someday. In the meantime, I have no choice but to protect your children and insure that they're kept out of Harm's Way." There was a thoughtful pause. "I don't expect that you'll ever thank me for this, but hopefully, someday you'll understand. Until then, as a father myself, I implore you to search your heart and commit yourself to a hospital that can treat whatever ails your mind, and make you well again."

Without another word, the judge stood and exited his court. There was silence. Dennis, Tracey and their respective attorneys each sat in shock. Dennis was not permitted to see his children for a period of one year. He cried whatever tears remained. At the very least, Tracey insured that he didn't cry alone.

Dennis walked aimlessly for hours before returning to the motel. He sat on the edge of the bed and stared at a TV screen of static. Christmas music drifted in from the bustling street, while flickering, holiday lights penetrated the white draperies. He reached for the nightstand, opened the top drawer and removed a bottle of pills. Pouring the yellow capsules onto the bed, he stared at them. His eyes began to leak. He walked to the bathroom and filled a glass of tap water. As he placed the glass on the ancient nightstand, he took notice of the telephone. With scarred wrists, he lifted the receiver and dialed. All three kids answered. "Hi! You've reached the Andersons. Please leave a message and we'll get right back to ya. Have a great day!"

He hung up and cried like a child. He reached into his wallet, removed a picture of the kids and dialed the phone again. Shane, Beth and Tyler repeated the same. "Hi! You've reached the Andersons. Please leave a message and we'll get right back to ya. Have a great day!"

Dennis stared at the photo. He dialed again.

"Hi! You've reached the Andersons. Please leave a message and we'll get right back to ya. Have a great day!"

He sobbed like a baby. "How did this happen?" he groaned, and then the first glimmer of truth came back.

He'd worked too late and was rushing to get home. The rain had stopped earlier, but the streets were still wet and slippery. He was thinking of Tracey and the kids, and driving much too fast for the conditions. And then he saw them. Two teenage kids in a beat-up Camaro pulled out from a poorly lit parking lot. Dennis hit the brakes so hard he thought his foot would bust right through the floorboards. It didn't. The car barely slowed. Just as his car struck the Camaro, the boy in the passenger seat stared straight into his eyes. Dennis couldn't imagine a more dreadful sight. The boy's expression was pure fear. The rest transpired in slow motion.

The awful sounds of broken glass and twisted steal preceded the screams of human pain. In an instant, the world lay still again. Dennis felt a dull throb travel the length of his body. He was hurt. No matter, he struggled to free himself from the wreck. It took a few minutes. In the meantime, he heard one of the teenagers moaning. He wondered why the other remained silent and forced himself out of the car.

The sight made his body convulse, and he fought back the vomit. The Camaro was no more than a heap of junk with two teenage boys trapped inside. While the boy behind the wheel cried for his life, he hurried to the driver's side door and pulled. It was no use. Hyperventilating, he peered into the car's interior. The passenger lay bent in half and motionless. Panic welled up inside Dennis. He pulled and pulled on the door. It wouldn't budge. In the distance, the sound of sirens grew closer. After one more futile pull, he collapsed to the street and fought for air. He felt like he was having a heart attack.

The Jaws of Life freed both boys, while the paramedics confirmed that they were alive. "I'm not sure the passenger will ever walk again," one of them commented, and then closed the rear of the ambulance. As the siren wailed toward the emergency room, Dennis grabbed for his chest. It just had to be a heart attack.

Dennis returned to the present and looked at the pills. "It's me," he whimpered. "It's been me." He swiped the pills onto the floor, looked at the photo of his kids and dialed home again.

"Hi! You've reached the Andersons. Please leave a message and we'll get right back to ya. Have a great day!"

The sound of his children's voices made him realize what was most important in life. Anger welled up inside him. "I have to stop playing the victim," he grumbled. "I'm the only one who can fix this." Anger was a better place than despair.

He dialed one last time, and listened. "Hi! You've reached the Andersons. Please leave a message and we'll get right back to ya. Have a great day!"

He hung up and walked to the mirror. Wiping his eyes, he peered into them hard. "It was a car accident! And you're going to let everything slip away because of an accident?" He shook his head. "I don't think so!" Hope had arrived, and not a moment too soon.

He quickly rummaged through his wallet and slid out an old, weathered business card. He picked up the phone again and dialed. A machine answered. "Hi, you've reached Brad Perry at Psychology Associates. Please leave a brief message and I promise to get right back to you. If this is an emergency, beep me at 555 1355. Have a great day!"

Dennis spoke slowly. "Hello, Mr. Perry, my name is Dennis Anderson. I think I need your help. When you get a chance, please call me at 555 4587. Thank you."

On the morning of January 11, 1996, Brad Perry admitted Dennis into a thirty-day voluntary detox program.

Dennis sat in a circle of recovering alcoholics and addicts, each one sharing details of the nightmares that landed them there. As one of the councilor's spoke of the glory found along the Twelve Steps, Dennis's mind drifted off.

He flashbacked to the morning at the sailboat slip when he and his children went sailing. He could picture them each donned in their bright orange life vests. It was a calm, sunny day, as he recalled, with a few clouds bringing about slight winds – a perfect day for Tyler to break into sailing. He envisioned the three children seated at the rear of the boat, listening attentively as he gave a lesson on safety and worked the sails. He looked up to see the animals foraging on the shore, the birds gliding in the sky – all which was natural and good in the world. He looked back to discover Shane entranced in the freedom of it all. "It's the feeling of freedom," he'd told him. "That's what you feel." Searching all three faces, he added, "But guys, you don't need to feel happy or peaceful to feel free. Like everything worth living for, freedom lives right in here." He pointed to his chest, and then inhaled deeply to drive his point home. The kids followed suit. He grinned, and began to work the main sail. The kids looked at each other, smiling. It was a glorious day.

Butch Pereira, a fellow alcoholic, tapped Dennis's shoulder – jerking him back into a cruel reality. "You alright, man?" he whispered.

"Yeah, thanks," Dennis answered, returning the whisper. "Did I miss anything?"

"Nothin' you won't hear a thousand more times in the next month." He grinned. "Looked like you were quite a ways from here, though. Where'd you go?"

"To where my kids are…or were anyway." Dennis stumbled on his words.

Butch picked up on the melancholy. As a display of genuine friendship, he risked being considered nosy. "You're not alone, pal. Can't wait to get back to 'em, huh?"

Dennis's eyes immediately welled up. "I wish," he said. "The judge took them from me. I'm not sure I'll ever be able to see them again."

"Whoa there," Butch interrupted. "Where's your faith?"

"Faith?" Dennis was taken aback by the simple word.

"Yeah, faith," Butch confirmed. "You honestly think this is the end of the line for us?" Before Dennis could reply, the man answered the question himself. "Nope. This is just another starting point, that's all my friend. Yep. You'll be with your kids again. Just by the look in your eyes, I can guarantee it."

"Well," Dennis said with a shrug, "you must see something I don't. But I pray you're right."

Butch grinned wide. "Sure I'm right. Besides, how can anyone take something from you when it lives right in here?" Butch slapped his chest.

Dennis's face went flush, goose bumps covered his body and

every hair on his body stood on end. Butch smiled like an angel sent from heaven; an angel who knew Dennis personally. In one moment in time, Dennis's faith was questioned and reinforced.

While Dennis learned the incredible effort it took to walk twelve steps, snow began to cover the ground. Shane and a group of boys chased each other around during recess in the school playground. Tommy Goodman, Shane's best friend and confidant, had spread the word that Shane's Dad was locked up in a "drunk tank." Jeff Frost, the yard bully, heard the rumor and approached Shane. "So, your Dad's gettin' dried out, huh?"

Shane's eyes watered and his hands trembled from anger and nerves. "Whad'ya say?" his voice quivered.

"I said your Dad's a drunken bum. And what are you gonna…"

Shane threw a right hook, landing square on Jeff's nose. Blood exploded from the boy's face. A circle quickly formed around them. "FIGHT," everyone chanted. "FIGHT!"

Through a pool of tears, Shane threw Jeff into a headlock. "Take it back," he yelled. "Take it back, Jeff, or I'll keep poundin' ya. I swear it."

Before Jeff could mutter the words, Mr. Curran, the science teacher, jumped in and broke them apart. He grabbed Shane by the arm and pulled him off his prey. "Shane," he panted. "What on earth's gotten into you?"

There was no response. Mr. Curran escorted Shane by the nap of the neck to the Vice Principal's office. "Well then," he said, "we'll just have to see what your mother thinks about you punching people in the face."

"I don't care what my mother thinks," Shane answered through his sniffles. "She doesn't care what happens to me anyway."

~ XI ~

Dressed in a pair of Westwood Hospital pajamas, Dennis peered through the fog of sedation. The scratchy sound of slippers dragging the floor led him into one of the many offices off the main corridor. Dr. Weiss, a staff psychologist, gestured that he take a seat. Hesitantly, Dennis did. Dr. Weiss was a kind-looking man. He opened Dennis's folder and wasted no time getting down to business. "Mr. Anderson, by signing yourself into our care, I truly believe that you've made the best decision."

"It's Dennis."

"What's that?" Dr. Weiss inquired.

"Please call me Dennis. I won't be able to confide in you if you call me by my father's name."

Dr. Weiss smiled. "Very well then. Dennis, I think you've made a wonderful step in the right direction. It may not seem that way today, but I can assure you – before you know it, life will return to normal."

Dennis's mind drifted off to the only thing that kept him breathing; his children. Beneath a shedding tree in their back yard, he and Shane shared a game of catch – both smiling contentedly to be in each other's company. "You keep throwing the ball like that," he told his eldest son, "and you'll be playing for the Red Sox before you know it."

Returning into the house, he found his youngest at the kitchen table, struggling with a math problem. In time, they worked it out together. "I'm telling you, Tyler. All you have to do is apply yourself and someday, you'll be flying the space shuttle for NASA." The boy believed.

Dennis knelt beside Beth in her pink bedroom. Together, they spoke to God. He tucked his little girl into bed, pulled the covers under her chin and finished the nightly ritual with a kiss. "Sweet dreams, Princess," he said. "Sweet dreams, Daddy," she answered, and everything in the world was exactly how it should be.

Dennis's mind eventually wandered back to the present where he found Dr. Weiss sitting on the desk before him. The man's hand was actually resting on Dennis's shoulder. "Dennis?" he asked, softly.

"Huh? Oh yeah, I'm sorry. I was just thinking about my kids."

"And I'm sure there's no better place for your mind to be," the kind doctor said. "However, for the time being, we need to concentrate on what's going on with you, so we can get you back to them. Okay?"

Dennis shook his head in embarrassment. "I'm sorry, Dr. Weiss. I…"

"It's Ken."

Dennis looked up, puzzled.

Dr. Weiss smiled. "If we're going to cut out the formalities, then let's do it all the way around." Ken Weiss extended his hand. Dennis took it. "The name's Ken and it's my pleasure to meet you." They shook firmly. The psychologist asked the only obvious question. "How do you feel?"

Dennis finally got the chance to hit the release valve on his pressure cooker. He talked with the shrink for two solid hours about his living hell. "Most of the time, it starts with cotton mouth. I can't swallow and feel like a giant pillow has been lodged in my throat. All at once, my heart starts beating rapidly and my chest becomes constricted – as if an elephant is standing on it. I get sweaty palms, quivering knees, trembling hands, and tingling in my extremities. My breathing becomes quick and shallow. Although I try to stop it, I hyperventilate. Then, the worse happens, and it feels like it comes right from my very core." Dennis paused to collect himself.

"What is it," the doctor prodded.

"They're incredibly strong feelings of impending doom which increase to a point that's unbearable. I feel like I'm having a heart attack, or worse, going crazy. My thoughts get all jumbled and hazy. I become lightheaded, drunk on fear, and knowing this makes me feel like even less of a man. The adrenaline rush is so intense. But I look out onto a world where there is never anything to attack, or run from.

Realizing this makes everything even more confusing. Afterwards, I always feel 'off.' And though I don't want to, I become anti-social and go inside myself for answers I can never find."

Dennis took a few more moments. The doctor's eyes were both compassionate and patient. With a deep breath, he went on. "Even when I'm in the middle of a full-blown attack, I'm more afraid of the next one that's sure to come. Each one is complete anguish, torment, and inner torture. But the anticipation is even more crushing, making me avoid people and places where my wicked secret might be revealed. Now, this mask of normalcy that I wear has gotten so tight that I'm depressed most of the time. It's a living nightmare, a horror show. I feel like some invisible monster is chasing me. But I can't take it anymore. I'm tired and I need it to stop." He began to cry. "My kids…" he whimpered, and couldn't manage another word.

Beth knelt by her bed, her hands clasped tightly together. Tears streamed down her beautiful, little face. She prayed aloud. "Dear God, I know I probably don't talk to you as much as I should, but I really need to talk now. God, I'm so sorry for bein' bad sometimes. My Mom has to yell at me and my brothers because we don't listen, or we don't finish our chores. But God, I promise – if you let my Daddy come back home, I'll never be bad again. And I'll make sure that my brothers will be good, too." Tears cleansed her face completely. "We'll eat everything in our plates. We'll go to bed on time. And we won't ever talk back again. Please, God! All we want is our Daddy back. That's all we want. If you do that for us, then we'll be the best kids you ever saw. Honest."

Beth blessed herself, stood and walked to the window to await her Daddy's return. As she peered out onto the darkness, the reflection of her tears was caught in the glass. "Please, God," she whispered. "Let my Daddy come home. We miss him so much."

There was a scream from the other room. It was Tyler.

Tracey was hovered over her youngest when Beth entered the room. Tyler was hugging his Mom and crying. Shane lied on the top bunk, his hands folded behind his head. Tears ran down his red cheeks. The Anderson family, as they once knew it, had been destroyed.

"Tell Mamma," Tracey whimpered. "What is it?"

Tyler hyperventilated. "It's Daddy," he explained. "I keep dreamin' about him. I keep…" Violent sniffles caused him to stop.

"I know, Tyler," Tracey whispered. "I know it hurts. Go ahead, get it out. There's nothing wrong with crying."

"I keep dreamin' that Dad's not comin' back," Tyler stuttered. "I keep seein' him runnin' far away from us. It's dark and he keeps runnin' and runnin'."

Tracey locked her embrace. "No, Ty," she promised. "Dad didn't run away from us. He'd never do that. It's just that he's sick and needs time to get well. Then he'll come back." She looked for Shane and Beth. "You guys know he'll come back, right?"

"When Ma?" Shane asked, sarcastically.

"Just as soon as he's well again. I promise."

"But Daddy promised, too," Beth wailed. The pain was evolving into anger. "Daddy promised that he wouldn't leave – THAT HE'D NEVER LEAVE!"

Beth stormed out of the room in tears. Tyler clung to his mother. Shane placed his hands back behind his head, doing all he could to be the man of the family – doing all he could to remain strong.

One endless month passed and Tracey was still seated at her desk, slouched over. The weight of the world rested on her shoulders. Pete approached and grabbed her by the hand. "Okay, okay, the doctor's here. Want to go for a cup of coffee?"

As they walked, Tracey filled him in. "I honestly don't know what to do, Pete."

"About what?"

"Dennis finally got himself into therapy. He's at Westwood."

"Good for him," Pete said. "It's about time."

"The problem is, I got a letter from him yesterday and it's addressed to the kids."

Pete cringed. "Uh, Oh."

"Exactly. If the court finds out about it, Dennis will get sent to jail for violating the no contact order."

"What did it say?" Pete asked.

"I couldn't even bring myself to open it."

"So, what's the big deal?"

As if he were insane, Tracey glared at him. "The big deal is that I honestly don't know what to do with it." She shrugged. "Pete, I have no idea how long Dennis is going to be there. If I let the kids read it…"

"You can't let the kids read it."

"Yeah, that's what my mother says."

"And she's right. Hey, I know it sounds cruel, Trace, but if I were you I wouldn't get the kids' hopes up."

"That's what I was thinking. They've just gotten to the point where they can function somewhat normally again. I'm not sure it would be smart to jeopardize that."

Pete nodded in agreement. "I know it stinks, but you have to keep it from them. I'd hold on to it and give it to them when all this craziness blows over. "

"See, I'm not sure I should do that either. They'd hate me for keeping their father from them. They already feel…"

Pete grabbed her hand. "You're not keeping anyone from them. You're protecting them from more pain, that's all. I'm sure they'll understand when they get older."

Tracey nodded. Her face showed signs of relief. "I just hope he doesn't keep sending them. It's tearing my heart out."

Dennis was seated across from Dr. Ken Weiss. They were in the middle of another session, and he still felt incredibly depressed. "It's been six weeks," he moaned. "And they haven't responded to one of my letters. I'm afraid to call."

"And you shouldn't," Ken advised. "That would definitely be a bad idea. Even as far as the letters, I'm not sure it's such a great idea."

"Ken, do you mind if I ask you something?"

"Of course. Anything."

Dennis proceeded, cautiously. "How is it that I've been sitting in this chair for weeks spilling out my guts, while you just sit there and listen – and tell me nothing."

"What do you mean – tell you nothing?"

"You've never told me what's wrong with me."

As if he'd completely explained it to his patient before, Ken sat shocked. He leaned forward, folded his hands on his desk and spoke softly. "Dennis, I'm sorry. I thought it was evident. You've been diagnosed with depression and Post Traumatic Stress Disorder, or P.T.S.D."

Dennis sat in disbelief. Ken elaborated. "From what I can tell, you've been clinically depressed for at least five years. How this was initially brought on is still unclear to me. Sometimes it's just a chemical imbalance that takes place in the brain. Sometimes, it's hereditary. Does anyone in your family have a history of depression?"

"I don't know. I was orphaned as a baby and adopted when I was five." He shrugged. "I suppose that's why being a good, dependable Dad has always been so important to me."

"Perhaps," Ken said. "I'm sure we'll get into it." He breathed heavy. "As far as the P.T.S.D.: After the car accident, your anxiety level became so heightened that the panic attacks took over – so severe that it's been nearly impossible for you to function normally. But with medication…"

"I'm screwed," Dennis mumbled.

"No, Dennis. You're not screwed. You're just sick."

Dennis's eyes welled. Ken walked around the desk and comforted his patient. "Dennis, listen to me. All the problems that you've suffered in recent months are not your fault. They're really not. You have to start to believe that."

Dennis looked up, but didn't believe. He was riddled with guilt.

Ken patted his shoulder. "It's not your fault, Dennis. Losing the job. Blowing up at Tracey. Being separated from your children. Even the attempted suicides. You're not to be blamed for these things. I'm telling you, we have to get rid of the guilt before you can heal."

Dennis was too busy crying to respond.

"Although millions of Americans suffer this same plight," Ken explained, "many don't even know they have it. Or, for reasons too many to count, many more refuse to investigate. 'Just nerves' some say, and try to alleviate the sharp slaps of panic with alcohol or sheer force of will. Of course, as you've learned, either attempt escorts them deeper into the bowels of their own hell."

Dennis nodded. Tragically, he knew only too well.

"Dennis, the real question has never been whether or not you're sick. It's really about what you're planning to do with your illness."

"What can I do?"

"You need to start taking medication, no questions asked. We can start you on Lithium and monitor the dosages for effectiveness. And, if you give me a solid nine months to work through a rigorous treatment plan, I guarantee that the worse of it for you will be over."

Dennis squirmed. "Nine months?" Panic worked its way back into his heart and mind. He thought about so much time being separated from his children and the tears rolled faster. Then, as if he reached a place called acceptance, he softly muttered, "Then what?"

"Then I'll go to court myself," Ken promised, "and testify that you are one of the most loving fathers that I have ever met, and that it would be an absolute injustice to your children that they spend another day without you in their lives."

Dennis nodded. Through the tears, he agreed to the medication and an intensive, nine-month treatment plan. The tears, however, were now filled with the first glimmer of hope.

Ken broke out the contract. "Dennis, let me make this clear. Once you sign this contract, you'll be mandated to stay on the hospital's premises for the entire nine months. If you leave for any reason, I will not be able to help you...or testify on your behalf." He slid the contract toward Dennis and offered his pen. "It's important that you understand what this means."

Dennis had no choice. Without the doctor's testimony, the court would tear him to pieces. He grabbed the pen and signed.

~ XII ~

The long months of separation were enough to break the coldest heart, or test the strongest faith.

At Westwood Hospital, Dennis finished writing another letter and dated it, February 28, 1996. He folded it up, sealed the envelope and gave it a kiss. The letter was addressed to Shane, Beth and Tyler Anderson.

The term panic disorder was repeated over and over. Amazingly enough, Dennis was still reluctant to believe. He was no coward. He'd never panicked in his life. He'd been taught to be a man, to handle any situation before him. *Was he really so much weaker than he'd believed?* With a gentle, logical voice, Ken Weiss calmed him and explained. "Ironically, in some strange sense, you've always been right. Your problem is physical. It's a chemical imbalance in the brain." He prescribed Xanax and suggested meditation.

Dennis was still afraid. If he'd learned anything, he now understood that there was a long road ahead. A panic attack was what happened to other people – until it happened to Dennis Anderson.

Meds made Dennis feel apathetic, almost unable to function. Suspended in a sea of thick syrup, life became surreal. He felt increasingly more detached from everyone and the reality they experienced. With each pill popped, he only wanted to sleep and escape forever.

As Dennis and Tracey struggled to adjust and overcome in their new worlds, the weeks ticked by.

At a banquet hall, Tracey received a coveted journalism award for uncovering fraudulent activities at City Hall. She beamed with pride. Her mother and sister were seated at her table. They embraced her with the support deserving of any hard-working, single parent.

Dennis stood in a line at Westwood. A nurse handed him a paper cup containing two pills. He tipped the cup to his mouth and drank from a water fountain to wash them down. The room was filled with souls in much worse shape than he. He was more groomed and starting to feel healthier.

Frustrated, he'd tried to overwhelm the attacks through vigorous, insane regiments of exercise, or other attempts at releasing large amounts of adrenaline. It definitely helped, but unfortunately, he also learned that his will was an ineffective weapon against this ruthless enemy. Just by thinking of the symptoms, he'd start to feel them, so he spent much of his time trying to avoid such thoughts. This, of course, only forced his mind to visit them often and begin the vicious cycle that he couldn't cease. Even when the symptoms were starting to be taken under control, this proved a daunting task.

Spring had finally arrived when a set of training wheels were set on the Anderson's thawed lawn. As Tyler tried balancing a two-wheel bicycle, Tracey ran behind him. Shane and Beth looked on. All three kids were happier, and there was even a little laughter in the air. "Not bad, Ty," Shane said, "but when Dad taught me, he…"

A dirty look from Tracey halted the comment. Beth ran into the house, crying. The others were left to face a horrible moment of silence. Tracey felt like crying. It was hard enough to juggle work and raising kids alone, but when there was bitterness and anger involved, it sometimes felt unbearable.

Dennis learned that although he suffered terribly, he did not suffer alone. In a fast-paced, stress-filled world, the number of panic sufferers was staggering, epidemic. Oddly enough, he felt some relief with the company. He started to take the time he usually spent worrying and used it to gain such knowledge. Before long, he learned that he had to venture within himself in order to heal. It was a journey only he could make, but at least now he knew that he wasn't alone in making it.

Each night, he knelt beside his bed and prayed with all the

strength and conviction he possessed. Once finished, he blessed himself, grabbed a framed photo of Shane, Beth and Tyler off the nightstand and kissed his children goodnight. Lying in bed, he worked out many of his problems in the solitude. *Tracey never cheated on me*, he finally understood, and began to miss her, too.

Many moons passed before Beth had finally reached the age to take gymnastics. During a routine maneuver, she slipped off the horse and fell hard to the matt, breaking her arm in the process. Instinctively, she screamed out in pain. "Daddy!"

Tracey rushed to her aide. "Oh God, baby. I'm here."

"I want Daddy," Beth cried. "I want my Daddy."

As summer approached, Dennis took a leisurely stroll through the Westwood grounds with Ken Weiss. They laughed over a shared joke. Dennis was starting to feel more like himself. A small stack of letters protruded from his back pants pocket.

Dressed in his cub scout uniform, Shane reported to a church basement. All in all, it turned out to be a good night. As Tracey arrived to pick him up, though, the Scout Master made a stinging announcement. "Just a reminder people: Next month, we'll be camping out for our annual father and son weekend."

Shane stormed out past his mother. Tracey caught up to him in the parking lot. "If you want, Shane, I'm sure it would be alright if I went."

"No!" he yelled. "It's for boys who have fathers." The tears began. "And I don't have one of those anymore."

Dennis was extra anxious at one of his therapy sessions and reminded Ken of his legal battle. "My court date is quickly approaching and I know I can't leave, but…"

Ken nodded. "I'll call the court and explain."

In the meantime, the formal classes on anxiety disorders taught Dennis many things: The horrid condition of panic disorder transcended all barriers; race, religion, economic. No one could ever forget the first time they stood face to face with this sadistic demon.

The relaxation exercises seemed so much like childbirth classes that at first, Dennis thought them a waste. Still desperate for peace, however, he stuck with them. Thank God! With one hand on his belly, he learned to watch his abdomen rise and fall with each breath. He never realized it, but it had been years since he breathed from his diaphragm.

After learning the value of affirmations, transcendental meditation had him chanting one-syllable Mantras, while he breathed in and out like a baby. He'd tighten each muscle in his body, and then allow them to relax. He did this until his limbs felt like rubber bands and the rest of him felt submerged in Jell-O. The instructor whispered, "Imagine the safest place in the whole world. Now, imagine a staircase that leads down to this wonderful place. There are ten stairs. As you descend each step, you will breathe in deeply and exhale, feeling more relaxed with each step down."

Dennis said the word ten in his mind, took a deep breath and imagined stepping down. Nine, he thought, took in a deep breath, exhaled and stepped down. He was definitely more relaxed. By the time he hit the number one, he felt paralyzed, serene. There was no longer a need to think, just be.

For twenty glorious minutes, he imagined spending time in his favorite place – adrift on a sailboat with his three children. When it was time to return, on cue, the instructor helped him breathe his way back up the staircase.

Slowly, he opened his eyes and smiled. Though the trip had taken him through more than a solid year of hell, he'd finally returned with the answer. With all the responsibilities, the obligations and the important things he needed to remember each day, he'd forgotten to breathe.

Before she knew it, Tracey stood before the judge who'd imposed the one-year restraining order. The judge checked his watch and shook his head, realizing that Dennis would not be showing. Heavy rains banged angrily against the windows.

The man finally looked up from his bench, leaned down and spoke softly. "Mrs. Anderson, I think the restraining order remains in the best interest of your family for another year, or until your husband decides to show some interest."

Tracey held back the tears. "You think so?" she whimpered, but still wasn't ready to give up. "Your Honor," she said, "maybe he's just late because of the weather."

"This is already the second call," the judge sighed. "He's not coming, Mrs. Anderson."

Tracey nodded her head slightly, while the judge signed a document forbidding Dennis from his children for an additional year.

Dennis stood alone in the middle of the Westwood yard. The rain drenched him from head-to-toe. He checked his watch and the tears began to mix with the weather. He tilted his head toward the sky. "Please God, help me go home," he yelled. There was no choice but to honor Dr. Weiss's contract. Though he couldn't leave, he wanted nothing more than to bust through the front gates and sprint all the way to the courthouse. But he'd learned the hard way. He had to do it right this time.

Tracey returned home and finished writing a letter to Dennis. She signed it, *your loving wife, Tracey.* After proofreading it, though, she crumpled it up and threw it onto the floor. She collapsed onto the bed, grabbed Dennis's pillow and hugged it. The tears rolled on.

Though he'd counted every tormented minute that it took to get there, Dennis sat with the new friends he'd made at the hospital and ate Thanksgiving dinner. He had a soft spot in his heart for these people, and was starting to look more like staff than a patient. Another letter stuck out of his rear pocket. His stay was winding down.

Without much warning, Christmas arrived. Four stockings hung over the Anderson mantle where a row of family photos once smiled. Any reminder of Dennis was too painful. Tracey and her Mom did their best to make it a magical holiday, but something was missing. Even Beth, faithfully standing sentry at her window, couldn't find it. Santa proved to be more generous than ever. It was one of the few perks of living within a dysfunctional family.

Dennis dreamed he was standing in a long, dark tunnel of depression and asked himself, *What if it's one more step?* In the blink of a blinded eye, the smallest ray of light penetrated the blackness that consumed him. Cautiously, he stood and slowly walked to the light. With every step, the light's intensity increased and he ran. The brightness warmed his face and for the first time, he could smile. Reaching the end of the tunnel, he looked back. Although it was a pain that would linger in his memory, at last the brutal maze had been conquered. He awoke panting and looked around. The answer was simple and had been with him throughout the entire journey: Hope had always been the only escape.

The nine months were finally up, and alas, Dennis was a free man. He felt great, but was more than anxious to reunite with his children. It was dusk when he reached a pay phone. He called Chuck Robertson at home. The New Year had just passed. It was 1997.

"Hello?" Chuck answered.

"Hi Chuck. It's Dennis." He cleared his dry throat. "Dennis Anderson."

"My God, Dennis. How are you?"

"With the exception of not seeing my kids for over a year," Dennis answered, "I've never felt better."

"Great. Glad to hear it." There was an awkward pause. "What can I do for you, Dennis?"

"I need to see my kids, Chuck. I really do. How soon can we get back in court to make that happen?"

"Ummm…Dennis, I don't mean to pee on your parade, but I'm not sure this is the best time to file a motion."

"What?" he snapped. "I've spent more than a year doing everything that was asked of me and you're going to tell me I can't see my kids?"

"Dennis. Dennis. I understand. Don't get upset. Just hear me out." The compassionate attorney cleared his throat. "I think it's wonderful that you've gotten help; that you've gotten well again, and so will the judge, but…"

"But what?"

"But you've spent an extensive period of time estranged from your children. And, I'm sure that time was equally difficult on them. The way the court is going to see it, is that…"

"CHUCK, PLEASE!" Dennis was losing it.

Chuck lowered his tone. "Dennis, hear me out on this, okay? You know I would never steer you wrong, especially where the kids are concerned. You know that, right?"

"I'm sorry, Chuck. Go ahead."

"The court is going to consider the time that you've spent away from the kids, Dennis. The judge is going to weigh the value of their adjustment toward living without you against having you re-enter their lives."

"So you're telling me that I'm never going to see them?"

"No. No. Not at all," Chuck promised. "What I'm saying is that the judge will be looking for stability on your part. After nearly a year of hospitalization, he's going to want to see how you interact in society. You're actually going to have to prove you have the ability to maintain a safe, loving and consistent relationship with your children before the court will ever entertain a reunion."

"And how do we prove that I'm capable of that?"

"By establishing a secure residence, gainful employment and an active role within the community. You might even consider attending religious services."

"How long? How long do I have to prove myself before we go back?"

"Give it six more months, Dennis. Six months away from inpatient treatment; time that would more than prove your credibility to the court."

"Okay, Chuck. Okay. I'll stay away. I'll get established and call you in a few months. Then…"

"Then I'll fight hard for you and get those kids back into your life, okay?" Chuck's tone was firm.

"Thanks Chuck." Dennis paused. "And let's keep this conversation confidential, okay?"

"Sure, Dennis. But wouldn't Tracey feel better if she knew."

"Not yet, okay?"

"Okay, Dennis, Mum's the word. But please, don't mess up now. Stay clear of the kids until we get permission from the court."

"I know. I know. They won't see me until the court allows it." Dennis took a deep breath and exhaled slow. "Thank you Chuck, for everything. And tell Anita I send my best."

~ XIII ~

In the elementary school auditorium, Tyler sat on the stage, along with eleven other children his age. A spelling bee was in full swing. Mrs. Crawford, the English teacher, fired one word after the other at the nervous kids. Two children had already been eliminated before Mrs. Crawford reached Tyler. "Tyler, the word is ELEPHANT," she said slowly.

Tyler's forehead wrinkled. "ELEPHANT," he repeated. "E L E." There was a breathtaking pause. "P H A N T. ELEPHANT."

"Correct," the excited teacher announced.

From the rear of the auditorium, one person began clapping and only stopped when no one followed the lead. Hushed giggles traveled through the crowd. Tracey turned to her mother. "Looks like Ty has a big fan," she whispered.

Joyce smiled and waved at her grandson. "More than one, I'd say."

Dennis walked through the front door of the boarding house with some take out food and a newspaper. He wore a uniform with the name *DENNIS* embroidered on the front and *COLLISION TOWING* stitched on the back. He sat down at an old, rickety kitchenette table and sipped from his coffee. *May 30, 1997* was the date on the front of the paper. He circled a few possibilities in the classifieds. Once done, he fingered through the paper before coming upon an article written by Tracey Anderson. He read it and grinned. After cutting out the piece and folding it up, he pulled out the classifieds. He picked up the phone and dialed.

"Hi. Bob Naughton, please?" There was a brief wait. "Bob, Dennis Anderson here. I was over at New Dimensions for some time." He smiled. "Right, I'm the guy." After another deep breath, Dennis took the plunge. "Bob, I see you're looking for a new gun slinger over at your firm."

It was a glorious night when Beth made her debut as a dancer. The recital hall was packed with proud parents and heckling siblings. Tracey and the Anderson entourage were seated up front. Halfway through the show, Beth trembled from nerves. She was scheduled to perform a solo. The lights went down, the music up, and Beth tap-danced her way straight into the hearts of a delighted crowd.

As the house lights went up, a cameraman wearing a hat and bifocals pointed his 35MM at her and clicked off several shots. With a wink, he whispered, "Beautifully done, Princess." The stranger took one last photo, and then walked away.

Beth felt goose bumps. She bowed twice, but as the curtain was drawn, she scanned the crowd for the cameraman. "It can't be," she whispered under her breath.

Dennis was impeccably dressed and felt a jolt of adrenaline surge through his body. It was similar to panic, but different enough to actually enjoy. While his colleagues at Naughton Advertising filled the conference room, he shook off the jitters of presenting his first proposal to the new company. He was at the bottom of the food chain again, but he couldn't be happier. "Ladies and gentlemen," he announced, "allow me to introduce the new look for Harvey's Super Stores."

He removed a sheet from the giant easel, revealing a colorful collage of drawings and catchy phrases. The room erupted in cheers. Harvey Patterson, the client, clapped the loudest.

After an impressive presentation, the room cleared out. Bob Naughton and Harvey Patterson, however, stayed behind.

"Dennis, since we opened the very first store back in 1978," Harvey said, "I've entrusted all of my advertising to this firm. To be quite honest, though, this is the best material I've ever seen. I couldn't be happier." He glared at Bob. "Whatever you're paying this guy, Bob, it can't be enough."

With a wink for Dennis, Bob replied, "It's funny you should mention that. I was planning to offer Dennis a position where he can run his own creative team." He looked Dennis square in the eye. "So, what do you think?"

Dennis shook his boss's hand. "I think I've finally returned to a big part of my life. I accept. Thank you."

It was opening day on the baseball diamond. Shane took the pitchers mound; prepared to use all the moves his father had taught him. As the crowd cheered him on, he struck out the first three batters. He then got on deck to hit. As he approached the plate, Tracey yelled, "Come on, Shane. You can do it!"

Shane didn't even acknowledge his mother's screams. Instead, he concentrated hard and fouled the first fastball off into the woods. The umpire waited several moments for one of the younger spectators to throw the ball back onto the field. It never came. Finally, the ump plucked a new ball from his pocket and handed it to the catcher. The game resumed.

On the second pitch, Shane caught all of it and tagged it over the fence for a solo home run. While rounding the bases, he searched the many different faces in the crowd. Although everyone was smiling, he just couldn't bring himself to do the same. The only person he wished had seen the homer was his Dad.

It was a Sunday afternoon when Dennis arrived at the soup kitchen of Our Lady of Grace Church with a dozen adolescents. He had become heavily involved in the Youth Group. While other adults took the kids on outings to have fun, he opted to show the teenagers that some of the greatest joys in life could be found helping others who could never return the goodness.

He rolled up his sleeves and began serving potatoes to the homeless and downtrodden. He smiled at each one, occasionally sharing a laugh with some. And while he did his part, Sarah Olson, one of the teenagers from the Youth Group, said, "Mr. Anderson, I have a strange question."

"Then prepare yourself for a strange answer."

She giggled. "Seriously though – why is it that being here makes me feel better than almost anywhere else I've ever been?"

Dennis smiled. "It's actually quite simple, Sarah. There's no better feeling than having purpose and that's exactly what you feel when you're here." He drifted away in thought. "Just wait 'til you have kids. I swear there's no better feeling in the world. With a grin, he returned to the present and looked into Sarah's face. "I've found that the greatest reward we can give ourselves is to give to others. Trust me, I've learned the hard way."

Dennis continued to spoon out more than potatoes. He offered love and compassion to those who needed it, while teaching others to do the same. Life was becoming purposeful again.

Dressed in a new suit and tie, Dennis took a seat near Attorney Chuck Robertson when Tracey entered the courtroom, alone. She took a seat. Dennis glanced at her, but quickly looked away when their eyes locked. Chuck picked up on it. "Maybe you should talk to her."

Dennis shrugged, while a grin forced its way into the corner of his mouth.

"All rise," the court officer announced. "This court is now in session, with the Honorable Judge Evelyn Sabra presiding."

Judge Sabra looked over the paperwork before her, and glanced thoughtfully at Dennis. "Mr. Anderson," she said, "from what our records indicate, you have not seen your children for a period exceeding two years. Is that correct?"

Dennis stood. "It is, Your Honor."

"And you have come before the court today to appeal an active No Contact order that currently prevents you from visitation?"

"Yes, Your Honor, I have." He shook from nerves. "If I may speak?"

The judge gracefully waved her hand, giving him the floor.

He breathed deeply and poured out his heart. "Your Honor, two years ago, I was convicted of Domestic Assault for which I admit I was guilty. Though I will never be proud of that fact, only in the last year have I been able to understand why I acted as I did." He took another deep breath. "You see, Your Honor, I have been diagnosed with depression and P.T.S.D.; two debilitating diseases that destroy the lives of many people. To this, I can attest: I have lost my career, my home, my marriage, but worse of all – two years of my children's lives; time which can never be retrieved." The tears were unlocked. "I can't imagine that receiving the death penalty could have felt any worse. I am sorry for what I did, but I think I've been punished for my illness long enough. I have paid dearly." He paused to ponder the harsh penalty. "Your Honor, in the past two years, I have done everything that the court has asked of me and then some. In truth, my greatest motivation to overcome my illness and reclaim my life has been my children. Without them, I might as well have been put to death by this court." More tears began to fall. This time, Dennis didn't try to stop them. "More than my own soul, I love my kids. I love them and I beg this court – regardless of the circumstances or conditions set before me – please allow me back into their lives again, back to where I've always belonged. I was sick once, very sick and I understand that there was a need then to protect them. But no more! I'm not sick anymore. I take my medication. I have proven to be a productive citizen in our society." He paused one last time before the big finish. "Most of all, Your Honor, I believe my children and I should be reunited because I was never just their father – I've always been their Dad. You see, I know in my heart that they need me just as much as I need them. Please, Your Honor, let me see my kids. Let me love them again in ways that they can understand. PLEASE!"

With the exception of several sniffles, the courtroom remained silent. Tracey cried the hardest. The judge shook her head. This one simple act struck fear in Dennis's heart. As if he were about to be electrocuted, he squeezed the arms of his chair.

"Mr. Anderson," the judge explained, "your passionate plea has touched the heart of this court, but you must understand, the welfare of your children is pinnacle."

Dennis nodded. He felt ready to pass out. Tracey slid to the edge of her seat.

"Mr. Anderson," the judge continued in her smooth tone, "I apologize for the pain and suffering that you have endured over the past two years. It's quite evident to me that you have suffered tremendously."

Dennis nodded again, but awaited the worse.

The judge smiled at him. "I apologize," she said, "because although I agree that your children needed to be protected at a time that you required psychological help, I'm not sure that a No Contact order was in the best interest of anyone involved – you or your children." She looked at Tracey. "It also appears that you and your children have not been the only victims of your illness."

Dennis's eyes leaked with joyous tears. The judge actually possessed compassion. He looked at Tracey and smiled.

"You see, that's the problem with family court," the judge said. "The laws are vague and those passing judgment are forced to play it safe. It's a complete disaster all the way around." She shook her head, disgustedly. "From my experience, families and court just don't mix – especially in Family Court. The judge looked over the paperwork once more and made a notation. She looked up and revealed her decision. "Mr. Anderson, I am going to grant your appeal and revoke the No Contact order."

Dennis nearly leapt from his skin. "Yes!" he yelled, impulsively.

"With several conditions," she announced. "That you reunite with your children under the initial supervision of the Department of Social Services." She smiled at Dennis again. "At least until your kids get used to the idea of having their Dad back in their lives. Some children need more time to readjust and we don't want to make another mistake by shocking them again."

"I understand, Your Honor." Dennis had to force the words past the lump in his throat. Tearfully, he smiled back. "Thank you, Your Honor. Thank you so much!"

The judge leaned forward and surprised the entire courtroom. "No, Mr. Anderson, thank you. You should be commended for placing the needs of your children before your own. Many fathers could learn from the love you've displayed to this court." She directed her next instructions toward Tracey. "The first visit will be scheduled for this coming Monday at 6:30 p.m. Will there be a problem with this, Mrs. Anderson?"

Dennis froze.

"No. Not at all," Tracey squeaked. She, too, was overwhelmed with emotion. "I'm absolutely delighted, Your Honor."

For the first time in a very long time, Dennis stepped into Tracey's eyes. When he did, Tracey returned the gaze and stared straight into his soul. She smiled sweetly. He swallowed hard. There were still deep feelings. Tracey's eyes never left her husband's. "And I know the kids will be, too," she added. "They've really missed their Dad." Her face was awash in tears.

The judge smiled wide and returned her attention to Dennis. "Very good then. Mr. Anderson, on Monday at 6:30 p.m., you will be reunited with your children." The rest came out as *blah...blah...blah...*

Before the judge even finished her spiel, Dennis turned to Chuck Robertson and hugged him. He'd never been happier. He turned back toward Tracey and winked. She happily returned it.

Dennis thought back on all that had happened. As tragic as many of the twists and turns had been, he'd also learned a few invaluable lessons along life's crooked path: Each aspect of life was like a single domino. One of the tricks to keeping everything standing was to make sure that the dominos were spaced far enough apart. This way if one fell – the rest didn't have to come tumbling down along with it. It was amazing. One single event, no matter how simple and meaningless at the time, could very easily trigger a terrible chain reaction; a series of more events that could just as easily tear a life down to its foundation. The theory was simple. If one domino went down, then the best reaction was to concentrate on saving the others. Dennis thought about his car accident and shuddered. One twisted moment had been more than enough to spin his entire world out of control. Strangely enough, he still couldn't recall the morning that he awoke to discover all his dominoes lying on the ground. *We're each hanging on by a thread*, he thought. But he was standing in the sunlight again, and thanked God for all of it.

~ XIV ~

Dennis arrived at the Department of Social Services building at 5:30 p.m., one hour earlier than scheduled. He was excited and nervous at the same time. Lorna Foley, the DSS caseworker assigned to the Anderson case, met him with a smile. Curiously, Dennis had three shoeboxes tucked under his arm.

"A little early, no?" Lorna commented.

Dennis smiled. "Nope. Actually, I'm two years late."

Lorna chuckled and rubbed his arm. She was a compassionate soul. Without delay, she escorted him into a small conference room. "Why don't you take a seat right in there," she said. "The Men's Room is down the hall on your left and there's a soda machine right across from it, in case you get thirsty."

Dennis nodded, but his eyes kept leaving Lorna – scanning the hall for his children. He rubbed his sweaty palms on his pants and took a few deep breaths. Lorna chuckled again. This time, she kept her hand on his arm for a long moment.

"Hey, don't look so serious," she teased. "You're going to do fine." Her face turned serious. "Try to get comfortable. When your children arrive, I'll bring them right in. Fair enough?"

"Better than fair. Thanks." Dennis was beaming.

Lorna took notice of the boxes. "New sneakers for the kids?"

"No, just three pairs of shoes that the kids never saw me wear."

Lorna's forehead wrinkled. Dennis opened the boxes. She peeked in. Her forehead stayed wrinkled. She looked up at him for a second, and then back into the boxes. Suddenly, she gasped for breath and her eyes filled with tears. He smiled at her reaction. Lorna patted his arm one last time. He placed the boxes under the conference table.

"You're going to do better than fine," she whimpered. "You're going to do great!" She left, wiping her eyes and shaking her head the whole way.

Dennis sat alone, and spent the long minutes watching the second hand on the clock. He paced the floor and every few minutes, stuck his head out the door to check the hallway.

After checking the hall for the tenth time, he walked to the window and looked out. The kids were nowhere in sight. As he spun on his heels, the sight of Shane, Beth and Tyler standing in the doorway nearly dropped him to his knees.

He hurried to them, collapsed to his knees and opened his arms wide. The kids, however, were more afraid than excited.

"Shane, Beth...Tyler," he sobbed. "My God, have I missed you guys. Come give Dad a hug."

Sluggishly, the kids walked to him. Shane was the first to offer a half-hug.

"Hi slugger, how have you been?" Dennis asked.

Shane didn't respond and avoided all eye contact. Beth quickly took over for her brother and offered an even weaker version of a hug.

"Oh, Princess," Dennis cried. "Has Dad ever missed you!"

Beth giggled nervously which quickly turned into tears, sorrowful tears.

Tyler stood with Lorna Foley, half his body concealed behind the woman's leg. Lorna bent down to address the small boy. "Tyler, aren't you going to give your Dad a hug?"

Tyler began to hyperventilate until the real bawling began.

Panic struck Dennis's heart. He realized that for the young ages of his children, too much time had passed. A great distance now separated them. For a second, he didn't know what to say. Shane and Beth were staring at him like he was a ghost from the past – an unfriendly ghost. Dennis wiped his eyes and took a seat at the table. He gestured for his children to do the same. Reluctantly, each one sat. Lorna Foley remained in the doorway, trying to conceal her tears.

His tone was gentle. "Guys, I need you to know that I never meant to hurt you."

Shane, the man of the family, stood and cut to the chase. "You left us," he yelled. "We needed you and you left us!" The tears blinded him from trying to stare his father down.

Dennis shook his head. He desperately fought off the impulse to break down and weep. As if sifted through a wad of cotton, he explained, "No, Shane. I never left you. For the past two years, I know there have been times when you needed me, and I wasn't there." There was an emotional pause. "But I swear, I never left you."

By now, all three kids were weeping. Tears of resentment, longing, sorrow, confusion and anger came pouring from their eyes. Dennis took a deep breath, reached beneath the table and revealed three shoe boxes. On the top of each box, in big bold letters, were the names SHANE BETH TYLER. He slid each box over to its rightful owner. The kids looked confused.

"No," he repeated in a whispered cry. "I never left you."

Shane was the first to crack the lid on his box. His eyes grew wide. He reached in and pulled out a giant pile of letters bound by a thick rubber band. He looked around and found Beth and Tyler holding the same size pile. He began fanning through his pile, taking note of the many dates. He looked at his brother and sister, and then at his Dad. Before he could ask for them all, Dennis explained. "Once I got to the hospital to get well again, I wrote you guys every day. I was going to mail them to the house, but the judge explained that I'd get in more trouble if I did. So I decided to hold on to them until we could be together again."

"You wrote us every day?" Beth asked.

"Every day," Dennis confirmed. The tears were coming fast now.

Still entrenched in bitterness, Shane pulled a baseball from the box and looked at it. Again, before he could say anything, Dennis explained. "This past season, fourth game in, you guys played the Tigers."

Shane swallowed hard. "Yeah?"

"Second inning," Dennis continued, "before you smashed the longest home run I've ever seen in my life, you fouled a ball off into the woods."

"Yeah, I remember," Shane said. "The ump stopped the game, but no one ever found the ball."

Dennis's eyes filled to the point that he couldn't see. "There was no way they could, Shane. I caught it."

Shane's body began to convulse. He tried to remain strong and dove back into his box, only to pull out wrapped Christmas gifts, two Birthday cards, and Easter candy, everything he believed his father had missed. The entire box was filled with his father's love.

Beth removed two photos from her shoebox. "These are from my dance recital," she said. "I remember a man taking these, but he…"

"Was wearing a funny looking hat and moustache?" Dennis asked.

Beth nodded and began to cry. "Oh, Daddy."

"You smiled right at me, Princess. And you never looked so beautiful."

Tyler held one of the treasures from his shoebox. He looked up at his father. Dennis laughed. "That's a program from your Spelling Bee, Ty."

Tyler was still having a tough time understanding. "You were there Dad?"

"I was. And I learned that you've been eating too many artificial snacks since I've been away." Dennis laughed again. "C.H.E.E.Z.E.?"

Everyone laughed, especially Tyler. The small boy looked at his older brother and sister. "Dad saw me, too," he squealed.

"And I was never so proud of you! There's nothing wrong with second place, Ty." Dennis beamed with pride. "I could tell that you studied hard."

The kids retrieved copies of their report cards, more letters, cards and photos from their shoeboxes. Each box was a complete account of the last two years of their lives.

Finally, Shane stood and approached his sobbing father. "I'm sorry, Dad. I'm so sorry."

Dennis grabbed his son and pulled Shane to him. Dennis hugged the boy tight, allowing his son the opportunity to let out all the pain. Shane bawled like a baby. "Shhhh," Dennis whispered. "You have nothing to be sorry for. I'm proud of you, son. You took good care of our family while I was away." He looked into Shane's eyes. "But it's time for you to be a kid again, okay?"

Shane grinned, and nodded with relief. He still couldn't respond through the sniffles.

"I'm not sick anymore, guys. Dad's back and I'm never going away again."

Beth and Tyler followed their older brother's lead and swarmed upon their Dad. Dennis was smothered in hugs and kisses. He wept openly with his children; weeping for the time they'd lost and the opportunity they'd been given to start over. "Nope, the days of feeling sorry are over," Dennis cried. "Even when I couldn't be with you guys, I never left you. I was always with you. Always! Because you live right in here." Dennis slapped his chest and took a deep breath. His children did the same, and then smothered him in more hugs.

By fall, Dennis and his three children drifted out on the lake. There were no other boats on the water. Everyone was beaming with smiles. Life was good again – nearly returned to the way things had been two years before. Even Tyler was wearing his white sailor's hat.

"You guys are too much," Dennis chuckled. "I'm telling you, we're just going to dinner."

"Sure, Dad," Shane teased.

"Yeah, sure," Tyler echoed.

Beth jumped in. "I don't know, Dad. Mom bought a new dress and she's been starving herself for two weeks to fit into it."

Dennis blushed. The kids picked up on it. In chorus, they sang, "OOOOOH!!!"

Dennis tried to return to seriousness. "Guys, don't get your hopes up. A lot's happened."

Shane nodded. "But a lot more good things happened before you got sick, right?"

"Geez, I don't know." Dennis was at a loss.

"Come on, Dad, where's your faith?" Beth asked.

Dennis froze and his breathing became shallow.

He flashed back to the Stepping Stone Detox Center where Butch Pereira, a fellow alcoholic, tapped him on the shoulder – jerking him back into a cruel reality. "You alright, man?" Butch whispered.

"Yeah, thanks. Did I miss anything?" Dennis said, returning the whisper.

"Nothin' you won't hear a thousand more times in the next month. Looked like you were quite a ways from here, though. Where'd you go?"

"To where my kids are, or were anyway." Dennis never hesitated with his response.

Butch picked up on the melancholy. As a display of genuine friendship, he risked being considered nosy. "You're not alone, pal. Can't wait to get back to 'em, huh?"

"I wish," Dennis said through the tears. "The judge took them from me. I'm not sure I'll ever be able to see them again."

"Whoa there," Butch interrupted. "Where's your faith?"

"Faith?" Dennis was taken aback by the simple word.

"Yeah, faith. You honestly think this is the end of the line for us?" Before Dennis could answer, Butch answered the question himself. "Nope. This is just another starting point, that's all my friend. Yep. You'll be with your kids again. Just by the look in your eyes, I can guarantee it."

"Well," Dennis said, "you must see something I don't. But I pray you're right."

"Sure, I'm right." Butch smiled and dropped the hammer. "Besides, how can anyone take something from you when it lives right in here?"

Butch slapped his chest.

Dennis's face went flush, goose bumps covered his body and every hair on his body stood on end. Butch smiled like an angel sent from heaven; an angel who knew Dennis personally. In one moment in time, Dennis's faith was questioned and reinforced.

Dennis looked up to find his three beautiful children grinning. Shane patted him on the back, pointed to Beth, Tyler and himself and said, "Yeah Dad, if we could start over, who says it can't happen to you and Mom?"

Dennis offered each of his children a hug. "Nobody says, that's who. I suppose we've all learned that anything's possible, right?"

Tyler saluted. "Aye, Captain. Anything." Tyler slapped his chest, causing the rest of them to do the same.

While Dennis sat amazed at the many spiritual signs, Shane cleared his throat. "Dad," he said. "We got you something. A welcome home gift."

Dennis smiled.

Shane turned toward his little brother. "Go ahead, Ty. Give it to him."

The young boy reached into his pocket, retrieved an old dirty bottle cap and handed to his father. It was the very treasure they'd buried many moons before.

Dennis's eyes swelled with love. He lifted the bottle cap and peered into the eyes of all three children. "Thank you, guys. I'll keep it forever."

Each of them beamed.

As Dennis struggled to regain his composure, he stood and began working the main sail. "You guys ever hear of a place called Gooseberry Island?" he finally asked.

All three children shook their heads. "No, Dad," they said.

Dennis smiled. "Then let's sail over there and discover it together."

He and his children laughed well past the setting sun. They'd learned that theirs was a love that could never be destroyed.

The End, Part I

Higher

A pair of wide-eyes search the unfamiliar playground,
as the giggle of captivating innocence turns to a squeal.
Seated upon a swing, a young boy looks back, begging,
"Push me higher, Daddy!"
With only a few pumps of his legs and a set of strong,
but gentle hands behind him, his fears are conquered
and he steps into the sky.

A pair of eager legs march into adolescence,
tripping on the discovery that the world can be unkind.
Again, looking back, those same eyes betray his silent plea,
"Push me higher, Dad!"
The labored hands of love take his desperate grip
and lead him on his chosen path.
Still, the sky is within reach.

A pair of old, tired arms long for a hug that has died,
as two feeble legs buckle at the knees.
With weary eyes, he looks toward heaven and whispers,
"Push me higher, Father!"
A pair of stronger, more loving hands lift him up
and carry him home.
For eternity, that sky shall be his carpet.

– Dennis Anderson

Part II
Gooseberry Island

"Don't be so serious…it's only life!"
–Captain Eli

~ I ~

Located on the East Coast, Gooseberry Island is a magical place where tourists flock in the summer, but where God resides year-round. Fashioned after Martha's Vineyard, the community is still small enough to be quaint. Lacking any industry or technology, the stars shine brighter here. As a result, most dreams are cast from the water's edge – where heaven meets earth.

And this is where the story takes place…

It was dawn. Two silhouetted men stood in the soft light of a cloud. Through the veil of fog, the taller man handed the other a thin book and patted him on the shoulder. The book was the approximate size of a menu. God was having a conversation with David before sending him into the world. The shadows remained faceless. There was a faint sound of birds chirping and the whistle of wind.

Gently and loving, God told him, "This is your life, my child. Order whatever you wish, but keep in mind – whatever you choose to taste you must finish."

David nodded anxiously and started flipping through the menu. As he read, God continued in a serious whisper. "And know also that others have made their own choices." There was a pause. "Choices that are different from those you will pick."

"I understand," David replied, though there was no way he could. He looked down at the menu and his excitement took over. "Whatever I wish?" he asked.

God's tall silhouette nodded. "Yes."

"I want the love of family and friends," David recited from the menu.

"That's fine," God interrupted. "But first your gender."

"Huh?"

"The spirit has no gender," God explained, "but on earth, you must either be a man or a woman."

"A man," David announced quickly. "I want to be a good

119

man...named David." He shook his head in confirmation. "After King David. I've always loved the Psalms."

"Me, too," God agreed.

"I want to be a man who creates things and knows compassion," David hurried.

"Granted, but not before experiencing pain and suffering," God answered.

David looked up and quickly thought about it. "I'll accept pain and suffering for compassion."

God nodded.

"I also wish to have commitment and wisdom and..."

"Good choices, David. But not before conquering trials and tribulations."

David looked up from the menu. "And courage?" he asked.

"After overcoming fear."

"Honor?"

"Once you have faced shame."

"Success?"

"Much failure," God answered.

David stared at his master, closed the book and handed it back. "I can't have any of the good without the bad, can I?"

"Sure. It's called love and no matter what you do, I'll always love you," God promised. "The rest, you see, must be earned. Pretty clever design, isn't it?" He placed His great hand on David's shoulder. "You're given one life, David. Don't you want to experience all that I've created; experience everything that you'll create yourself?"

"I do," David responded, trusting and robustly.

"Very well then. You shall taste it all. But before your journey begins, you must tell me your purpose."

"I don't understand?"

"What shall be the reason for your human experience?" God asked, patiently.

There was a dramatic pause. "More than anything," he answered with great joy and confidence, "I want to find my soul mate."

God embraced David and kissed him on the cheek. "Savor the feast, my child," He whispered, "and know in your heart that I will always be with you."

David took three steps and looked back. "Will I remember…you know." He pointed around the cloud. "Any of this?"

God offered a gentle and loving nod. "For a short time, yes, but the memories of home fade with the progressive measurement of time on earth. You will not remember any of this until you return to me. No one does."

"And what about death?" The nervousness grew in David's voice.

God shook his head. "The idea doesn't exist except in the imagination of mortal man. Once your purpose has been met, and you have lived out your life on earth, you will simply return home to me – to eternal, unconditional love." He gestured with His mighty hand. "Now go experience it all, as I too will experience it through you."

David bowed his head.

"Don't be so serious, David," God chuckled. "It's only life."

David stepped out of the cloud.

It was morning when a young mother and father held their newborn son in the maternity ward. As they stared with wonder into the boy's chocolate brown eyes, tears rolled down their cheeks. For a moment, the baby stopped bawling and gazed back into their eyes. The card taped to the glass bassinette read *David Alexander McClain*.

David got baptized, and the first years on earth whipped by.

On newly found legs, David, the curly-haired toddler, ran down the beach toward his father's open arms – straight past a sign reading *GOOSEBERRY ISLAND*. The tiny boy's mother knelt on an outstretched blanket, emptying a picnic basket and preparing the family's lunch. The father scooped the child into his arms and tossed him into the blue sky, catching him each time. Laughing at their playfulness, the mother finally summoned them to lunch.

In the background, a black fisherman mended his nets. Occasionally, he looked up at the McClain family and smiled.

In another blink of an eye, while his parents lovingly watched on, David received his first communion.

At eight years old, David stepped up to the plate with the number two pasted to the back of his jersey. With fear in his eyes, he faced the pitcher and waited. He swung once and then twice until finally catching a piece of one and dribbling it toward the shortstop. He ran like lightning and made it to first base safely. As he turned to the crowd, he noticed his parents jumping up and down, applauding. A great sense of relief washed over him. He blew out a huge breath, rolled his eyes and looked toward the sky in appreciation.

At 14 – as he would for the rest of his days – he knelt by his bed and prayed to God. After blessing himself, he turned in for the night.

At 16, David stood with the other male wallflowers at a school dance, and stared at a girl in a pretty polka dot dress who was already dancing with a boy. As he watched, the young couple began kissing. He couldn't take his sad eyes off her. While one boy after the other summoned the courage to ask different girls to dance, David stood alone. It was either the girl in the pretty polka dot dress, or no one. Though other girls showed interest, the one he already knew to be sensitive and kind hypnotized him.

~ II ~

It was early spring. David had just turned 26 when he and his girlfriend Allison were driving along a coastal highway in his convertible. It was late dusk, the beginning of their date. Allison applied the finishing touches of makeup in the rear-view mirror, and liked what she saw. David didn't even notice. He was too busy gazing at the stars above.

"What a perfect night to lie on the beach and count the stars," he said, revealing the depth of his thoughts.

Allison was still in the mirror. "David," she blurted, "you said you were taking me dancing."

He never paid her any mind. He was too distracted. "Ever wonder if there's other life out there," he asked, "you know, maybe even making wishes on our sun?"

Allison finally removed herself from the mirror and shot him a look. The look asked *ARE YOU SERIOUS?* He never noticed. "Come to think of it – no," she said, cynically. "No, I've never wondered that." She looked at her nails. "But I have wondered why this nail polish looked red in the store and now it doesn't," she snickered. "This stupid purple doesn't even match my shoes."

David returned to the present and looked blankly at his shallow girlfriend.

"Davey?" she asked. "What would you think if I got a boob job?"

He considered the idea and half-grinned. He was definitely attracted to her physically. It was the emotional end that she could never satisfy. Without a word, he shook his head and turned on the radio.

Allison realized she'd receive no response to her question and returned to the mirror.

David scanned the channels until reaching a station playing soft rock. He left it there and looked back toward the sky. Allison finished her makeup, pushed the rear-view mirror back toward him and switched the radio to pulsating techno music. He looked at her. She smiled, oblivious to the rude gesture.

"Have you ever considered that it might be nice for once to spend a quiet night together?" He looked back toward the sky and shook his head. "We could talk until the sun came up." He began daydreaming aloud. "Share our pasts, our dreams...what we really want for the future."

"I'd rather dance."

David was taken aback. "You'd what?"

"You heard me," she said, with equal amounts of vanity and crudeness. She looked at him and attempted compassion. "Truth is, Davey...I hate talking with you. You're too intense and it depresses me."

He was even more shocked. "What?"

She looked the other way and breathed heavy. "I hate this part," she mumbled under her breath, and then turned her body to face him. "Maybe it's good that we have this talk now, before you..."

"Before I what?"

"Before you get too attached." She took a deep breath and the rest came out in a blurt. "It's not working, Davey. I just want to have fun. I'm young."

He chuckled, cynically. "Young? You're almost thirty."

The comment made her snap. "Fine! But I'm old enough to know I don't love you."

Instinctively, he pulled the car off to the side of the road. The moon shone brightly on them both. "You don't love me?" he squealed.

Her face was incredibly smug. "Well, all you ever do is babble about faith and dreams and finding some soul mate." She shook her head. "You're worse than a girl."

He felt like strangling the conceited girl. Instead, he threw the shifter into drive and sped off. Allison looked sorry for the last comment, but not enough to remain quiet. "I think it's time we play the field and see other people," she suggested.

David was hurt. "Alli," he said, "I'm not sure there's a whole lot of field left for you to play."

She didn't get it.

David looked at her for a long time and within seconds; his anger was replaced by a smile. A minute later, he felt ready for laughter. He realized she'd just done him the biggest favor ever.

She didn't know what to make of the change in facial expressions and became nervous. "I'm sorry, Baby," she whispered.

"Don't be, Alli," he said. "Don't be. You're so right that it's actually hilarious. When I think about it, I'm not really in love with you either." He shrugged. "Maybe just the idea of being in love."

Allison felt hurt. "Look, I'm just not ready to settle down," she explained. "I know I'm not the right one…" She slid toward him, and whispered, "but maybe I could be the right one for tonight?"

David pulled the car into her driveway and threw the shifter into park. He looked back toward the sky. "Tonight isn't enough for me anymore, Alli." He shrugged. "Take care of yourself."

Shocked by the sudden breakup, she got out of the car and shot a longing look back at him. With a smile of relief, he pulled out of the driveway – leaving her to pout like the spoiled brat she was.

On the highway, he punched numbers into his cell phone. "Coley, it's Dave. Where are you?" He grinned and rolled his eyes. "Right. Where else would you be? I'll be there in ten minutes." He listened to his friend and shook his head. "No. Nothing's wrong. I just need to run something by you." He closed the cell phone and stomped on the accelerator.

Ten minutes later, David reached the Eagle. As he walked into the busy nightclub, he spotted Coley at the bar. His handsome friend was talking to an unsuspecting, female victim. David stepped up and yelled his drink order over the loud music. Coley noticed his friend and whispered something into the girl's ear. She giggled, nodded at David, and then walked away. David looked at Coley and shook his head. Coley smiled. With beers in hand, both men turned and placed their backs against the bar to face the action. David was out of his element. Coley was right at home.

"What'd you tell her?" David asked over the music.

Coley grinned. "I said that we had business, but once I got rid of you…" He smiled and took a swig of beer. "I'd be back for her."

David shook his head and took a swig of his suds.

"So what drags you into my world?" Suddenly, Coley's face turned nervous. "The deadline on the DeSousa project?"

David hesitated. His entire body language was sad.

Coley panicked. "The blueprints are almost done. I just have to…"

"Relax," David interrupted. "It's got nothing to do with work." He took a look around, unsure whether he should go on. "I don't know, Coley. Maybe I came to the wrong place."

Coley sensed that the issue was serious and gestured for his friend to follow. "Come on," he yelled, and started through the crowd toward a quieter corner. David was right behind him. Once there, Coley continued. "Trust me, you've come to the right place. Now, go ahead. I'm listening." His grin was almost contagious.

Reluctantly, David reported, "Allison and I broke up tonight."

Surprise painted Coley's face. "You what?" he asked. "What happened?"

"For starters, she told me she doesn't love me."

Coley smirked. "And that's a problem?"

David shot a bad look.

Coley laughed. "How is it that the entire male gender is addicted to sex, but not you? No, you have to be addicted to passion." He grinned. "It makes us all look bad!"

"Buddy, I love sex just as much as anyone," David vowed, "but I don't love Allison."

The smirk returned. "So again, what's the problem?" He began counting on his fingers. "Neither of you love each other and you both love sex." With a nod, he solved the puzzle. "Yep. Allison should definitely be the one for you."

"She's not the right one," David said, flatly. He took a long draw off his beer and shrugged. "After a while, there has to be more to a relationship than just sex."

Coley was taking a sip of beer and nearly spit it out. "I don't get it. You guys seemed so attracted to each other."

David smiled at his friend's reaction. "I guess the passion that attracts you in the beginning is sometimes the flame that burns you in the end."

Coley looked confused.

David shrugged. "She loves herself so much that there'd never be room for me – or anyone else, for that matter."

"I can relate," Coley muttered.

David glared at his friend. "You're pathetic."

"No, just realistic." There was a pause. "Dave, not everyone feels comfortable swimming at the deep end of the pool. Don't be so judgmental. We each make different choices in life. That doesn't make any of us any better or worse. Maybe just a little less brave."

David pondered Coley's words and chuckled. "Wow!" he hooted. "For someone who can't handle deep…"

"I know," Coley interrupted, comically. "It's scaring me, too." He smirked. "I think it's you who's the bad influence."

Coley looked around the room and caught a pretty girl's attention. "Sad part is … they're all the same. You can't trust any of them."

"Hello Kettle, this is Coley," David joked. "You're black." After a long chuckle, he shook his head. "I don't know, buddy. I think you're wrong there."

Coley pretended to be annoyed. "Did you come here to tear me up?"

"I'm just messing with you," David laughed. "Seriously, I appreciate the ear."

Coley nodded. "Not a problem, partner," he said, and then searched his friend's face. "For real, you okay?"

David nodded, convincingly.

Coley looked back toward the dance floor and eyed up the pretty one he'd talked to at the bar. They exchanged a big smile. David snickered, playfully. Coley sighed. "In that case, my man, I've done all I can here." He took a long swig and finished with a grin. "Wish me luck. And if you need me, I'll be at the shallow end of the pool."

Coley headed back toward the dance floor.

"Try not to drown yourself," David yelled.

To David's surprise, Coley turned back and stopped. "My point exactly!" he said with a wink. "Not a chance." At that very moment, the swaying crowd swallowed him whole.

David rolled his eyes and looked up. "And this is the help I get?" He finished his beer, scanned the room once and shook his head. The promiscuous lifestyle was clearly not for him. He stepped out into the dark night.

~ III ~

At Half Moon Architecture, David reported to work early – very early. In fact, he was the only one at work; already designing building plans on a massive drafting board. The only light shown above his workstation. When Tish, the firm's secretary, arrived, she turned on the rest of the lights. "Mornin', Dave," she yelled across the floor.

David offered a half-hearted wave, but his eyes never left his work. His concentration was intense. Tish shook her head and chuckled. She was used to it and never took it as an insult.

Minutes later, the boss, Norris Tripp, arrived with his briefcase in hand. As he walked toward his office, he stopped and spent a moment over David's shoulder. Norris admired David's work.

"Are we ever going to get you out of the dark ages and on a computer?" he teased. "CAD would save you so much more time."

For the first time, David looked up. He smiled. "Designing anything on a computer is like challenging a five year-old to a game of chess," he explained. "It's just plain cheating." He looked back toward his work and smiled again. "This is art."

Norris laughed aloud, patted David on the shoulder and headed toward his office. "At your pace, Michelangelo," he added over his shoulder. "I have no complaints."

Just then, Coley walked through the door. Norris spotted him and raised his voice. "If only everyone worked so hard, AND PRODUCED HALF THE QUALITY!"

Coley swallowed hard and took a quick left into the coffee station. Norris shook his head. David laughed. A moment later, though, his head was right back on his work – his focus, drowning out the rest of the world.

At the end of the day when most employees had already gone home, David was still intent on his project. The progress was clearly visible. In his carefree manner, Coley sauntered over and peered over David's shoulder. "Another 18 hour day," he asked, "or do you want to go for a cold one?"

David emerged from his haze, but didn't register his friend's face for a few strange seconds. He stretched out his body. "No," he yawned, "to both." He thought for a second. "I need to run off some stress. I'm hoping to get in three miles on North Beach."

"Everything alright?" Coley whispered.

"I'm fine." He looked back at his work and revealed his secret. "The trick is to stay busy."

Coley shook his head. "You wouldn't have time for a full-time girl anyway."

"Trust me, I'd make the time," David blurted. His smile reappeared. "And speaking of time, where are we on that DeSousa Project? Norris wants…"

Coley checked his watch and exhaled heavily. "Alrighty then," he said, comically, "I guess I'll see you tomorrow." He rushed toward the door. "Bright and early," he concluded over his shoulder. In a flash, he was gone.

David chuckled and returned to his project for a few finishing touches.

David pulled up to the North Beach marina in his convertible and parked. Dressed in sweats, he jumped out – his running shoes still unlaced. On the water, a father and his three young children were sailing toward the island. For no particular reason, David waved. They all waved back. "Some guys have all the luck," David muttered under his breath.

On land, with the exception of a few sweater-wearing stragglers walking along the beach, Captain Eli was the only other person in the world. Aboard his run-down vessel, *SERENDIPITY*, the old black sea captain mended tattered fishing nets. At the bow of *SERENDIPITY*, David stepped onto the dock and visited with his old friend. "Afternoon, Captain."

Captain Eli looked toward the sky. The sun had just set and the dusk was warm with light. "In California, I suppose." He grinned.

David looked back toward the sky and chuckled. "Right." There was a pause. "Big catch today?"

Captain Eli never looked up from the net. "Nope. But the day's not through." He took a breath. "And you?"

David's tone was solemn. "Inches away from finishing the Biltmore Hotel. The boss couldn't be any more excited."

Captain Eli searched his friend's face. "Looks like you could be, though." He awaited an explanation.

"Same old story," David explained. "Actually…" He shrugged. "I guess it's the story of my life."

"Well David, if it's that bad maybe it's time to write a new story."

David looked up, surprised. Captain Eli was no longer smiling. David offered a friendly snicker. "And it would be that easy, huh?"

"Why not? It's your life." Captain Eli's words were a matter of fact.

"Or maybe it's my fate."

Captain Eli tilted his head and raised one eyebrow. Neither gesture indicated agreement.

"You don't believe in fate?" David asked.

"I believe that the good Lord gives us the perfect conditions to experience anything we ask for," Captain Eli answered. "It really becomes just a matter of choice on our end."

David was confused.

Captain Eli smiled. "It's simple. We ask. God delivers." He shook his head and sighed. "The complicated part is we either don't recognize the prayer when it's answered, or complain about the outcome of the very thing we asked." He stared at David – who felt uncomfortable with the extended eye contact. "What is it you want?" he finally asked his young friend.

David bent to tie his shoes, and buy some time. "I can't seem to find the right woman," he finally answered.

"So stop looking."

"No such luck," David joked. "That's just me."

Captain Eli still wore his serious face. "No such thing as luck," he vowed. "Like I said, it's a matter of choice."

"What's that?" The firm tone came as a surprise to David.

Captain Eli smiled and softened his approach. "David, if you can't imagine it, it can't be. We call our own shots." He looked toward the horizon and nodded. "Yep. We create our own experiences; everything that makes up who we are." He looked back at David with eyes that penetrated the soul. "If it were different, there would be no such thing as free will, right?"

David stopped tying his shoes. Captain Eli now had his complete attention. "So just ask and wait, huh?"

"I'd say it's best to ask and then give thanks before even getting your answer." He winked. "Now who could deny that type of faith?"

David nodded again, and then finished tying his shoes. He stood and stretched out for the run. "Thanks, Captain. I'll give it a try," he said. "And I hope the fishing gets better for you."

"For us both," Captain Eli quipped. His smile was angelic.

With his head spinning, David walked toward the beach and stretched once more. Just before taking his first stride, he paused and looked up toward the dark sky. "Thanks for bringing me the girl of my dreams," he said aloud. At a jog, he started down the beach.

Within minutes, his breathing became heavy, and he was just starting to find his rhythm when a pretty woman appeared in the distance. She was walking her Golden Retriever on the approach. With his labored breath building, they finally got close enough to offer each other a smile. He traveled another ten feet toward the girl when a seagull landed on the sand between them. Suddenly, her dog took off after it. David couldn't slow his momentum and tripped over the leash. To his instant humiliation, he was catapulted onto the sand.

Lindsey tried to conceal her laughter, but felt horrible at the same time. David looked up, angry. His initial reaction was to lash out. His face quickly changed, though, when he looked into her eyes. She was smiling. He returned it, and then pointed at the dog. "Maybe you should try feeding him dog food," he teased.

"I am so sorry!" she said. "Let me help you up."

While Lindsey struggled to take control of the leashed dog, she offered David her other hand. He took it and stood. His breathing was still labored. A moment passed before she giggled and looked down at her hand. He was still holding it. Attacking the awkwardness with humor, she shook David's hand. "Nice to meet you, too. I'm Lindsey."

David caught the joke and blushed. He pulled his hand away in embarrassment. "Oh, I'm sorry," he said, smiling. "I'm David."

As he brushed himself off, the two locked eyes and remained there for an extended moment. David was overcome with shyness. "Well," he managed past the lump in his throat, "thanks."

Although the dog was jerking her around, Lindsey couldn't stop smiling. Her eyes never left David's. He half waved at her and turned to resume his run. "555-3874," she blurted, and couldn't believe that she'd given her number so easily. But she couldn't help it. Something electric, even magnetic, made her want to see this stranger again.

He stopped and turned. "What's that?"

She blushed. "555-3874. If you can remember the number, call me and I'll buy you dinner for the trouble we caused." She looked down at the dog and smiled. "I'll even keep Simon at home."

David was frozen and didn't speak. His mind raced. Unless his instincts were completely off, she was the 'plain Jane,' earthy-crusty type who valued that which could not be seen by the eye. With her wild hair and bright eyes, she was perfect.

Her smile grew wider. There was definitely a mutual attraction between them. She broke the silence again. "I don't want to keep you from your run."

"Oh…yeah." He looked down at his clothes and shrugged. "Don't worry about that. I just got started." He couldn't stop smiling either.

She nodded. He stepped forward and bent to pet Simon. The dog growled. Lindsey was shocked. "Simon, stop that!" she yelled at the Retriever. She looked up at David. "He never acts this way," she swore. She jerked the leash once and brought the K-9 under control.

David chuckled. "Sounds good," he said, "but I buy the ice cream." He looked down at Simon. "And maybe we should leave the big boy home for the first date."

Lindsey smiled. He was already contemplating more than one date. David stepped backward. "I'll call you," he promised.

"I'm counting on it. Just don't forget the number." Her eyes sparkled.

With a giant grin, David took off down the beach. Lindsey never flinched. She stood motionless and watched him as he ran away.

"555-3874," he repeated as he ran. "555-3874."

That night, from the comfort of his bedroom, David picked up the telephone and dialed.

"Hello?" Lindsey answered.

"Hi Lindsey. It's David."

"Oh hi! I was just thinking about you."

"You were?" He was already blushing.

"Uh huh," she muttered. "I was hoping you would call tonight."

He smiled. "What do you think about dinner at Capriccio's, then maybe catching a movie at the Columbus Theater?"

"Ummm, that sounds good, but…"

He panicked. "You'd rather go dancing?"

"Not at all," she chuckled. "I was thinking that we could get a dozen clam cakes from the BaySide, then take a long walk on the beach." She had the voice of an angel. "Maybe even just sit and talk?"

It was too good to be true. "Even better," he said. "Tomorrow night at eight?"

"Sure, but seven would work better."

"Then seven it is. Where should I pick you up?"

"602 State Road. Just beep and I'll…"

"I'll see you at your door tomorrow at seven," he graciously interrupted.

"Great," she whispered. "I'm looking forward to it."

David beamed. "Me, too." He hung up and looked at the phone. "You have no idea."

~ IV ~

The following morning at the Gooseberry Community Art Center, Lindsey beamed as she showed a child how to paint in watercolor. Her co-worker, Carissa Kennedy, noticed this and questioned it. "Someone's happy today. What gives?"

"I have a date tonight." Lindsey couldn't stop smiling.

Eager to know the details, Carissa pulled her away from her student. "Well, who is he?" she asked. "Where did you meet him?"

"I met him last night on the beach," she sighed. "Simon introduced us, and he's perfect."

"Perfect? What could he have possibly said to make you think that?"

"Nothing."

"Nothing? Then how do you know he's perfect?"

"By his eyes," Lindsey confirmed. "I know by his eyes."

Carissa shook her head. She was still unsold. "Linds, you're still new to the island. There are a lot of jerks here. Just be careful."

Lindsey looked at her friend with seriousness in her face. "I won't need to," she promised. "Not this time." The smile never left her.

David was hard at work on the drafting board, a smile plastered across his face. Co-workers walked by and took a second look. Some shook their heads. Others smiled at the difference in him. Coley finally approached him for the scoop. "What's up with you?" he asked with a smirk. "Got some lovin' last night, didn't you?"

David emerged from his work, looked at Coley and smiled. "I have a date tonight."

Coley patted his friend's shoulder. "That's my boy. It didn't take you long to get back in the game."

"Coley, what's the status on the DeSousa Project?"

Coley's face went flush. "Alright. Alright. If you didn't want to talk about, all you had to do was say so." He walked away, insulted.

135

David laughed aloud, checked his watch, and then returned to his work. The smile never once left his face.

Both David and Lindsey left work early. David cleaned his car, picked up flowers and got a haircut. Lindsey spent the same time getting herself ready.

It was nearly dusk when David pulled up to Lindsey's house in his convertible. With flowers in hand, he got out and approached the door. Lindsey's Mom, Emma, answered.

"Good evening, Mrs…ummmm."

Emma smiled and extended her hand. "Wood," she informed him. "Emma Wood."

David shook her hand. "Nice to meet you, Mrs. Wood. I'm David. And I'm here to pick up Lindsey."

Emma smiled and invited him in. "Linds will be right down. Can I get you something cold to drink?"

"No Ma'am, but thank you."

A man and woman entered the living room from the kitchen. The woman was smiling. The man extended his hand and introduced himself. "Hi. I'm Jacob, Lindsey's brother. And this is my wife, Sarah."

David shook their hands. "Nice to meet you both. I'm David."

They started with small talk and before long Jacob had David laughing. As Lindsey walked downstairs, David took one look at her and was removed from Jacob in mid-sentence. Jacob and Sarah caught this and exchanged a smile. David and Lindsey stared into each other's smiles until David remembered the flowers. He handed them to her. "Thank you," she said, and blushed.

Emma sauntered over, looked at David and smiled. "They're beautiful," she said, and reached for the flowers. "Why don't you let me put them in water, so you guys can get going."

Lindsey handed over the flowers, along with an embarrassed look to her mother. David smiled.

"Ready?" she asked him.

David nodded and said his good-byes to her family. They were obviously all very excited about the date.

He opened the car door for her and waved again toward the house.

Not thirty seconds down the road Lindsey turned to him and apologized. "I'm so sorry about the welcoming party back there. It's just that…"

"Please. Don't worry about it. Your family seems very nice. And your brother Jacob is something else. He seems so happy."

"Yeah, Jake's an incredible person. But believe me, he's had his fair share of sorrow." She caught herself and stopped. "David, I'm sorry. I shouldn't be burdening you."

David picked up on the depth and capitalized on the opportunity to open up. He placed his hand on hers. "Don't be sorry. I'm interested. Go ahead, finish."

She looked deeply into his eyes and went on. "A few months ago, we all moved here because of Jacob and Sarah. Their daughter, my niece Miranda, died from SIDS a year ago."

"Oh, I'm so sorry."

She nodded her appreciation. "Jake and Sarah took off for a while to heal. They came back and ended up talking me and Mom into moving to the most peaceful place on earth – Gooseberry Island." She shrugged. "So here we are."

"With Jacob's attitude," David said, "I would have never guessed."

"He is amazing. But if you asked him, he'd just tell you it's faith."

David noticed that his hand was still on hers, and started to pull away. She stopped him, intertwined their fingers and smiled.

It was almost sunset when they pulled into the North Beach marina. David looked toward *SERENDIPITY*. Captain Eli was nowhere in sight. It was unusual. Though Lindsey insisted on paying, David purchased a dozen clam cakes and two Pepsis from the Bayside Seafood Shack. Together, he and Lindsey sat quietly on a giant storm wall of boulders and watched the sun set. Just as the final sliver of sun went down for the night, David swallowed the last clam cake and looked at her. "Good show?"

"I can't imagine a better one," she replied.

They clasped hands again and started their walk down to the beach.

Hand in hand, they talked and laughed. In time, they took a seat in the sand. They talked about their dreams, their childhoods and even their fears. Lindsey took the lead on the conversation, while David took it all in. "Okay," she said. "You obviously have a great sense of humor. But how are you with serious?"

David grinned. "Try me."

"Ummmm, tell me one secret that no one else knows."

He was somewhat reluctant. "I love writing poetry," he finally admitted.

Her eyes lit up. She moved in closer to him.

"But no one's ever read it. And I'd really like it to stay that way."

"So you wouldn't even share it with me?" she teased.

"It's not that good."

She smiled. "And you're not a good liar."

He laughed. "We'll see," he whispered. "And now you. What is the one secret that no one will ever know but me?"

She gazed at the stars, comfortable in David's company. "I have this incredible fear of dying alone," she admitted. "And sometimes, I feel so lost – as if I don't belong."

He was shocked by the depth and moved toward her.

"I know it's silly 'cause I've never been alone." Her eyes were back on the stars. "But I still can't help the way I feel sometimes."

For the first time, they hugged. "It's not silly," he whispered. "And I'm glad you shared it with me." He pulled his arms away from her, peered into her eyes and smiled. There was unbelievable chemistry. It was as if this wasn't the first time they'd ever been together. They could both feel the connection. He stood, pulled her to her feet and led her down the beach.

At a certain point, they stopped. "Look over there," he said and pointed at the lighthouse to the north.

She did.

"Whenever you feel lost or alone," he explained, "all you have to do is come here. No matter how dark or stormy, that light will always guide you home."

She didn't know whether to kiss him or cry, so she did both. She wrapped her arms around him and kissed his cheek.

As the night progressed, they picked periwinkles in the moonlight. She kicked water at him. He took chase. At one point, they even lay on a patch of beach grass, staring up at the stars. "I've cast many wishes up there," she said.

He smiled. "I hope they all come true."

"Things are definitely looking up," she whispered and blushed when she said it.

He smiled, placed his hand in hers and looked back toward the sky.

Innocently, she rambled on. "I think God has done a wonderful job." She looked at David. "Do you go to church?"

"I used to." As if stalling for time, he looked around. "I love the message. It's the messenger that I have a problem with. I don't think the church of today was what God intended." He grinned. "Not that I can talk for Him."

Lindsey returned the smile. "You mean Her, right?"

He laughed.

"Actually, I don't think God's either," she said. "I believe that wherever there is love – that's God."

"I guess I'm not the only poet, huh?" He looked back at stars. "It's funny. I think these stars are the very reason I became an architect. I love the perfection in design, the raw beauty."

"David, the architect and the poet. How do you think that happened?"

"It's a mystery to me." He shrugged. "For some strange reason, I've always been drawn to writing it."

"Promise you'll show them to me."

"Why don't I just show you the one I write for you?"

139

The sun was just breaking the horizon when they realized they'd spent the entire night together.

"What time did you say your curfew was?" David teased.

"I didn't," she replied, with a mischievous grin. "I pretty much have forever."

He couldn't help it. He grabbed her and pulled her to him. Just before they kissed, he cleared his throat. "I promised myself I'd be a gentleman, but I don't know if I can stop myself from kissing you."

"David, trust me, you are a gentleman." She pointed to the sunrise and giggled. "If you're concerned with time, then this could actually be considered our second date."

He pulled her close and they kissed, passionately.

~ V ~

David and Lindsey each reported to work exhausted, but full of smiles. They had the whole day to dream about each other.

For once, David couldn't get anything done. Instead, he secretly wrote, hiding his work from everyone – especially Coley who constantly tried to peek. Though it was still early, the workaholic yawned one last time and left for the day. Co-workers looked at the clock, then at each other and shrugged. It was nothing shy of miraculous.

Lindsey spent the day in dreamland, alternating between smiles and yawns. Carissa asked for details. Whenever they could break away from the children, they ran off and spoke in excited whispers like two grade-school girls. Lindsey lasted the whole day at work.

As she approached her car, she discovered a folded paper stuck between her windshield and wiper blades. Smiling, she plucked the paper free, unfolded it and read:

Beauty
for Lindsey (only)

She radiates with the light of a thousand candles,
while her movements have the energy of a lightning storm.
The sweetest aroma lures even the strong,
though it is the scent of confidence that takes the kill.
With the giggle of an innocent child,
her tone is soft and gentle – almost heavenly.
She expects nothing, but her silence demands the best.
Her forgiving heart beats in the ears of all men,
yet it is her untamed spirit which screams out loudest.
Like a beacon in the darkest night, her comfort is safety.
Rarely revealing her deepest thoughts,

her words remain simple, for she is a mystery.
Her tender touch can be soothing or sensual,
as she is unconditional love-
both maternal and passionate.
In a word, she is beauty...
And you should see her on the outside.

Lindsey's face streamed with tears of joy. She held the poem to her chest for the longest time.

After a full night's sleep, David arrived at Half Moon Architecture early. He was rested, but cagey. He couldn't take it anymore. He picked up the phone and called information for the telephone number to the Gooseberry Community Art Center. He hung up, dialed the Art Center and waited.

"Community Art Center," Lindsey answered.

He smiled. "Lindsey Wood, please."

"David?" Lindsey asked excitedly, and then switched to a whisper. "I was hoping you'd call today."

"Miss me yet?" he asked in a similar tone.

"What do you think? I missed you before our date was even over."

"Me, too," he admitted. "When can I see you again?"

"Tonight. And I pick the place this time."

"I thought you picked it last time?"

She giggled.

"Okay, but should I be scared?"

"No," she whispered. "I want to take you to my favorite place in the whole world."

"Can't wait to see it. I'll be at your house at seven."

"See you in a few hours," she said and hung up.

The day's end found Lindsey driving, with David acting like a scared passenger. They laughed and held hands. Music played softly in the background. The sun was just going down for the night when Lindsey pulled into the marina near North Beach. It was the same place they met; the same place they had their first date. Captain Eli was aboard *SERENDIPITY*. He was smiling.

Though he was confused about the location of their date, David waved to Captain Eli and gestured for Lindsey to meet his friend. "Captain," David announced. "I'd like you to meet my friend, Lindsey Wood."

Lindsey smiled. Captain Eli climbed down from his boat and extended his hand. "Well, hello Lindsey Wood. Nice to meet you."

"It's nice to meet you, too, Captain. I hope you don't mind me saying..." She waited until he nodded. "I love your accent. It sounds so familiar, but I can't seem to place it. You're not from around here, are you?"

Captain Eli smiled. "I suppose we all came from somewhere." He searched her eyes. "But home for me isn't so far from here." He looked out onto the water. "Gooseberry Island is as good a place as any, though."

"I agree. I just moved here myself and absolutely love it."

Captain Eli nodded again, and then turned his attention to David. "David, I hope you're showing our new friend around the island. We wouldn't want her to get lost."

David nodded. As if the old sea captain had just said something profound, though, Lindsey felt startled. She searched the man's eyes.

He simply winked, and gestured toward the horizon. "I don't suppose you two want to spend such a beautiful sunset talking to an old seadog, now do ya?"

David and Lindsey looked at each other and smiled. Lindsey turned back to Captain Eli and offered the same smile. "Again, it was nice meeting you. I hope we'll see each other soon."

"I'm always here."

Lindsey nodded, looked at David, and then started running for the beach. "Come on, slowpoke," she called over her shoulder.

David waved to Captain Eli and took chase. Captain Eli smiled, contentedly.

The young couple ended up right back at the same spot they met. Lindsey stopped short and turned to meet him. He nearly ran into her. She opened her arms for a hug. "Well, here it is," she said, gesturing around with her hand, "my favorite place in the whole world."

It was the exact location of their first date. David understood and grabbed her face with both hands. After staring into each other's eyes, they kissed for a long while. She broke away first, anxious to tell him something. "At the risk of scaring you away," she said, "I…I need to tell you something."

He nodded, nervously. He was just as curious.

"I feel safe and comfortable and excited," she babbled. "I feel everything when I'm with you and I haven't stopped thinking about you." She quieted her tone. "I know this is going to sound strange to hear on a second date, but you're everything I've ever dreamed of, David. And you're going to think I'm crazy, but…"

He placed his finger over her lips and grabbed her hand, leading her to sit in the sand. As he joined her, he removed a piece of paper from his pocket, opened it and read, "One Favor. For Lindsey." He looked at her and smiled.

She kissed him. Her eyes were already filled with tears.

"You've lived within my sweetest dreams,
your voice, your smell, your stare.
And on the night an angel spoke,
I found you standing there.

Kindness, truth, a hint of love
betrayed within a glance.
As if I was still dreaming,
I prayed for just one chance.

For all the struggles I endured;
the wrongs I tried to right.
I always knew I'd walk through hell
to find you on that night.

And there you were- just smiling,
aglow with peace and love;
the answer to my every wish
I'd sent to God above.

I dare not ask for one more thing
from God – He's done His part."

He smiled and finished.

"From you, I beg one favor.
Please take care of my heart."

Wiping her tears, Lindsey collapsed to the sand and pulled him to her. Passionate kisses were shared through the night.

Many wonderful experiences ticked off the months of David and Lindsey's courtship.

They met each other's families over two comfortable dinner parties. They spent all the time they could down at North Beach. They shared picnics, flew kites, and played in the water like children. At the summer carnival, they visited a fortuneteller together and teased each other about the woman's vague predictions. They took long walks down the beach at sunset. And they fell in love more and more every day.

At the absence of Lindsey's relentless prodding, David finally gave her his collection of poems. "These aren't to be seen by anyone else," he said, seriously. "They're my deepest thoughts and I would never share them with anyone but you. They're way too personal." He searched her eyes. "Promise?"

She took the book of poetry. "It's our little secret."

She read through the table of contents. "The Past, Ice Cream Cone, Fields of Granite, Beauty." She looked up and kissed him. She returned to the list of poems. "In The End." He forehead wrinkled from curiosity. "What's that one about?"

As she scanned the pages for the poem, he answered, "My thoughts about death, or the impossibility of it."

She read the poem and her eyes filled with tears. "It's beautiful," she whispered, and kissed him. "You're beautiful."

The following morning, as Lindsey worked with the kids, a glow illuminated her face. Carissa sauntered over. "That smile is starting to make me sick," she joked.

Lindsey giggled. "I'm sorry. I can't help it."

"Does this guy really make you that happy?"

Lindsey was spellbound. "I've dreamt about falling in love my whole life and I knew it would be wonderful, but..." She sighed. "I never could have imagined this. I pray it never ends."

Carissa shook her head.

David stepped into Norris's office. For the first time in a while, he was all business. "We finally got you down to 40 hours a week, huh?" Norris teased in mid-conversation.

David smiled. "Yeah. It's been great." His tone was serious. He needed to clarify a piece of the future. "Actually, my hours are the reason I wanted to talk to you."

Norris looked concerned. "You want less?"

"No," David said, hurriedly. "I was hoping to take on more again."

"Really? Money problems?"

David grinned. "Future plans."

Norris smiled and leaned across the desk. "David, this business wouldn't be where it is today if it weren't for your work. Take whatever hours you can handle."

With a huge smile, David stood. "Thanks, Boss."

"Maybe it'll even scare Coley into giving me 40 good hours?"

"I doubt it," David laughed, and returned to work more hours than he'd ever worked.

~ VI ~

Unaware of the surprises he had planned, Lindsey was less than impressed with David's new career aspirations. For every extra hour he spent at work, she took the same time venting to her mother. And, it was getting worse.

Emma answered the phone. She listened for a few minutes before beaming with joy. "I understand. Mum's the word," she said. "But what a beautiful idea." She nodded her head, pulled the phone from her ear and yelled up the stairs. "Lindsey, it's David."

Lindsey ran down the stairs, grabbed the phone and received a big smile from her mother before she walked into the kitchen.

"Hi," she said and the rest of the time was spent listening and giving one-word answers. "Uh, huh." "Again?" "FINE!" The entire conversation made her frustrated and angry. She slammed the phone into its cradle. "God, I can't believe him," she shrieked.

Her mom returned to the room. "David?"

"Yeah. I swear he just did everything he could to pick a fight. Sometimes he says the most idiotic things." She shook her head. "I've hardly seen him in two weeks and it doesn't really seem to bother him. He says he's just been busy at work and can't break away, but I think it's more than that. He's been distant. I don't know how much longer I can put up with it."

Emma smiled slightly and patted her frustrated daughter's shoulder. "Don't get impatient. The best things in life are worth waiting for. Trust me."

"I don't know, Ma. Maybe he's the one that should be doing the waiting." She stormed out of the room.

Emma's smile just widened.

The doorbell rang. As she rushed to answer it, Lindsey nearly bowled her mother over. *It just has to be David*, she thought, *he'd never hang up angry*. Emma stood back, wiped her hands on a flowered apron and reclaimed her mischievous smile.

Lindsey tipped the young messenger and rushed the package into the house. For such a large box, it was surprisingly light. Under the watchful eye of her curious mother, she tore through the brown wrapping. The most beautiful dress she'd ever laid eyes on was hidden amongst the tissue paper. As she lifted the white lace into the air, a folded piece of stationary floated to the floor. She picked it up and read.

> *Baby Cakes,*
>
> *Sometimes I say things that I don't mean; hurtful things that I wish I could take back as soon as they leave my lips. Sometimes I get frustrated and angry, unable to understand where you are, but then I wish that I were right there with you. Sometimes I am stubborn and defensive, feeling as if I have lost control, but I must also remember to let go and trust. Sometimes I want to go to you, but for fear of rejection, I hold my ground and do nothing – and that has always been the wrong decision. Sometimes I don't listen as well as I should, failing to hear what you're really saying and I respond in ignorance.*
>
> *Lindsey, I love you and because I love you, I'll try harder to understand, to have more patience and to always admit when I'm wrong.*
>
> *I've been wrong...Forgive me.*
>
> *I saw this dress and thought of how beautiful you'd look in it. Please wear it tonight and meet me at Capriccio's. I can be out of work by 6:00 and I'll shoot right over. I can't wait to see you!*
>
> *David*
>
> *P.S. I really do love you, Lindsey!*

Lindsey wiped her eyes and caught her mother's grin. She smirked. "I'll be there. But this time, he's going to wait."

In spite of herself, Emma laughed.

It was almost 6:30 when Lindsey screeched into Capriccio's lot. She intended to be a few minutes late, but never expected it would take her so long to get ready. As much as she wanted David to wait, she also wanted him to gasp when he saw her. The valet attendant opened the car door, took one look at her and swallowed hard. She smiled. The extra time had paid off.

She expected the Maitre' d to escort her right to David's table. The older man smiled and handed over a dozen long stem roses. "Mr. McClain called and said he was running late. He said that the card would explain." Her mother's silly smile covered the distinguished man's face.

Blowing a wisp of hair from her eyes, Lindsey reached into the baby's breath and retrieved the card. It read:

> *Babe,*
>
> *I would say that I'm sorry, but those would just be words that you have heard many times before. This time, I'll say that I love you, a truth that you haven't heard enough, but one that lives within my heart. I do love you and I want things to be right between us. I want things to be good and happy and fun – with no need for excuses or apologies- only room for laughter and the whispers that we secretly share. Let's always remember our love and return to it every day!*
>
> *Meet me at the Eagle for drinks. I can definitely be there by 7:00. I love you.*
>
> *David*

Lindsey looked at Maitre d' – who continued to grin. "Did he say anything else on the phone?" she asked.

"Not exactly," the kind man muttered. "Just that he can't wait to see you."

"It certainly doesn't seem that way!"

As Lindsey reached the parking lot, she was surprised to find that her car hadn't been moved an inch. The valet attendant opened the door and smiled sweetly. "Best of luck," he said.

"Same to you," she replied, confused by the curious comment. Within ten minutes, she was at the Eagle.

The Eagle was much less posh and sophisticated than Capriccio's, but they served one heck of a margarita. Lindsey made a beeline to the lounge, grabbed a table in the shadows and checked her watch. She decided to give David ten more minutes. If he didn't show, she was leaving – home to contemplate the future of their strained relationship.

The bartender sauntered over. "What'll you have, Miss?"

"Margarita, no salt and a cup of ice on the side."

"Cup of ice on the side?" the man repeated. A silly grin danced across his tanned face.

"Yeah," she confirmed, her sarcastic tone reaching anger. If she didn't know any better, she'd swear she was playing the butt of some cruel joke. The man nodded once and turned on his heels. Lindsey checked her watch again. David had seven more minutes. Looking down at the beautiful white dress, she shook her head. *What a waste*, she thought, and could feel the tears fighting to break free.

Within seconds, the bartender returned with a bottle of champagne. The smile never left his face.

"I ordered a margarita," she roared and felt sorry for the attack before it left her lips. "I'm sorry," she added quietly. "It's just that my boyfriend was supposed to…"

"Meet you here at 7:00. I know. He called a few minutes ago and asked that I pour you a glass of champagne. He also asked me to give you this card." The man poured out the bubbly and handed her another of David's cards. With a wink, he was gone. Lindsey reluctantly opened it.

> *Sweetie,*
>
> *I would say I'm sorry for not being able to meet you just yet, but I'd rather say that I love you because only that – can define what I truly feel.*
>
> *Please bear with me! There are going to be times when other things might seem more important than you, but you have to trust that they're not. I love you more than anything in the world.*
>
> *I guess the rest is up to faith. I'll be at the Dockside by 7:30. I'm hoping more than anything that you meet me. Please be there…and bring the champagne.*
>
> *David*

Lindsey stood and noticed that every patron in the bar was gawking. She was right. There was a conspiracy. Her first thought was to go home and put an end to David's foolish game. Then it hit her. There was no way that David would have had the time to drop off both cards. This was something he'd planned. Looking back at the crowd, she smiled. This was something he'd planned very carefully. Her excitement made her legs start moving. Within minutes, she was in her car and speeding off to the Dockside.

As expected, David was nowhere to be found. Instead, a white stretch limousine sat idling in the front of the dilapidated shack. The chauffeur held a sign. It read *LINDSEY WOOD*. She cried when she saw it.

With her dozen red roses and bottle of champagne, she climbed into the back of the car. The driver offered a familiar smile and handed her a tiny card. It read, simply: *I knew you'd come. I knew you'd do what it took to find me. Enjoy the ride. I'm waiting. I love you! David*

Even though it lasted well over an hour, Lindsey enjoyed the ride. As the car slowed to a stop, for the first time, she stole a peek out the window. They were at the beach. David was waiting somewhere in the dunes.

The driver parked, opened the door and helped her out. "Have a beautiful time," he said. "I'll be here when you get done."

Lindsey felt like hugging him for his smile. She had seen it in the faces of so many different people all day. Something big was up and the quest was not yet complete. Grabbing her roses and champagne, she picked up her shoes and started for the ocean.

A path of small seashells glimmered under a full moon of light. It was obvious. Each had been carefully placed. They were the last clue on David's peculiar map. The row of shells looped and wandered through the shifting dunes until reaching several enormous conch shells. These were arranged in the shape of an arrow. Lindsey took a deep breath before stepping over the last dune.

The sight nearly pulled her to her knees. David was seated at a small round table right smack in the middle of the beach. He was dressed in a black tux and he stood when he saw her. Their eyes locked and even with the distance between them, Lindsey could see that his eyes were filled with tears. She hurried toward him.

On the table, with the help of a magical moon, a hurricane lamp illuminated two place settings, an empty vase and an empty ice bucket. Soft musical notes drifted on the gentle breezes, beckoning Lindsey to her thoughtful prince. Allowing herself permission to cry freely, she finally picked up the pace and sprinted.

As she reached him, she expected him to embrace her. He didn't. He dropped to both knees, grabbed her hand and blurted, "Be my wife, Lindsey. Spend the rest of your life with me."

Instinctively, she dropped to meet him in the sand. "Yes!" she answered through the sniffles. "I thought you'd never ask!"

David laughed and pulled her to him. "I love you," he whispered.

"And I love you," she countered before gesturing toward the

table. "And I love all of this. But why the treasure hunt?"

"Because I needed to be sure that you wouldn't give up on me when you weren't sure whether or not I'd given up. I needed to know that you loved me as much as I love you."

"Do you know now?"

"I do," he whispered.

"Good," she giggled, "because I'm not Simon – and this is the last time I chase you."

Between the laughter and tears, they kissed passionately – until he grabbed her hand and led her down the beach.

At the very spot of their first date, the same spot that she said was her favorite in the whole world, there was a huge sandcastle sitting in the dunes.

"Oh, David," she whimpered, and placed her face into his shoulder.

"Every princess deserves a castle," he said, and grabbed her face to stare into her eyes. "Linds, the reason I've been so busy is because…" He pointed to the land around the sandcastle. "I put a bid on this small patch of beach and the owners finally accepted it."

"You what?" she gasped.

"I want to spend the rest of life with you right here," he told her. He was completely choked up. "Falling asleep to the rhythm of the surf at your favorite place in the whole world. And if you ever feel lost again…" He pointed back toward the lighthouse in the east. "There's the light that will guide you home to me. Neither one of us will ever have to feel alone again."

She began babbling, but couldn't speak past the emotion.

"The sandcastle is only temporary," he whispered. "I'm going to build you a house right here."

She looked up in disbelief.

"Our foundation gets poured in the fall."

~ VII ~

The Woods and McClain families gathered for the celebration dinner. There was good conversation and laughter at the table. Everyone got along well. Even Simon was happy. Over dessert, Jacob leaned into David's ear. "A path of seashells?" he asked, and then slapped his future brother-in-law on the back. "You hopeless romantic."

David blushed and looked at Lindsey. She nodded. He turned back to Jacob. "I know Lindsey wants you to give her away, but I was wondering if you wouldn't mind staying up there with us as my best man?"

"I'd be honored!" he said, shocked. "But I thought your friend Coley would be your best man?"

"Coley and I have been friends for years. He'll understand. You're family."

Jacob smiled. They shook hands.

Lindsey turned to Sarah. "And since you're the sister I never had…"

"YES!" she screamed. "OF COURSE I'LL BE YOUR MAID OF HONOR!"

The girls hugged and everyone laughed at their affection. The dinner ended with a toast. With glasses raised, Jacob announced, "To David and Lindsey: Whether your path leads through sun or freezing rain, may you always travel it together. And may the Lord's guidance and all the love in this room go with you."

Glasses clinked. The young couple kissed.

David and Lindsey were married on North Beach at dusk – family and close friends in attendance to celebrate. Under the shelter of a white tent, the two exchanged their heartfelt vows, while the sun said goodnight on the horizon.

Hurricane lamps and candles lit the tent. David and Lindsey had their own table – identical to the one they shared on the night of their engagement. It was private and romantic, and the perfect spot to watch Coley chase girls all night.

At the end of the reception dinner, David called for everyone's attention by proposing a toast to his new wife. All glasses were raised. "To Lindsey," he said, "the love of my life. When you were born, the angels danced, and I feel like you were sent just for me – that we were born for each other." He peered hard into her tearing eyes. "I will love you forever."

After soft applause and sniffles, the music began. The entire song lasted one kiss.

Fall came quickly. At their house lot on North Beach, David and Lindsey shared a bottle of champagne, and watched as the contractor poured the foundation for their new home. The day proved symbolic of their relationship. As Simon ran around, David broke out the house plans for he and Lindsey to go over.

"There will be skylights located in each bedroom," he pointed out.

Lindsey was giddy. "To count the stars to sleep."

He nodded. "And a wrap around porch to face the lighthouse."

"So that we'll never feel lost again."

He shrugged. "Anything missing?"

"Maybe someone to fill the other bedroom," she blurted.

"What?"

She never embellished. Instead, she kissed him and poured out another glass of champagne. She then took a drink herself, avoiding the topic further.

He raised an eyebrow and smiled, but didn't question it further. They returned to the house plans.

Simon took chase after a seagull. David and his new bride shook their heads and laughed. *Thank God for Simon's fetish.*

After a long day at the construction site, they turned in for the night. As David began kissing Lindsey, she grabbed his face in both hands and spoke softly. "Hon, what do you think about having a child now?"

"Now? Are you serious?"

As if she just came up with the brilliant idea, she smiled and nodded.

"But we never talked about a child. We're building a house. You never mentioned it before."

"I know, but something's changed," she whispered, "and it's not about me wanting to have a child. It's about me having your child." She grinned. "I have this feeling that my life will never be complete without your baby."

David smiled and kissed her, passionately. They made beautiful love.

It was dawn when two silhouetted men stood in the soft light of a cloud. Through the veil of fog, the shorter man held a thin book the approximate size of a menu. David Jr. was having a conversation with God before being sent into the world. The shadows remained faceless. There was a faint sound of birds chirping and the whistle of wind. "There is a perfect plan for all people," God explained.

"But I'll still have to learn everything I already know?" D.J. asked, dumbfounded.

"Trust that everything you'll ever need for the journey, you already have inside you. The catch is – you can't remember it, or the experience would be compromised. There would be no reason to create what you already know will be, right?"

D.J. nodded, but was still confused. "But if I can't remember, how will I know the path I'm supposed to follow?"

"Intuition, faith, unmistakable signs. I will also send angels to guide you."

"How much time will I have?"

"Time is non-existent to me," God answered gently. "There are no promises. Some people live an entire lifetime in one moment. It's what you make it."

Nervously, D.J. inquired further. "What is the worse I can expect to encounter?"

"Feeling alone – which is the greatest irony in the universe. You are all parts of a whole and I am able to experience all I created through each of you. You are never alone – ever! Nothing would be more impossible."

"And there's no good without the bad, huh?" D.J. was still trying to make sense of it all.

God chuckled. "You remind me so much of your father."

"My father? I thought you were my father."

God pointed down from the cloud and showed D.J. his mortal father. David was happily going about his business.

"Your mortal father," God explained. "He, too, had many questions. And he asked for the same things."

D.J. looked down at David and smiled. God noticed it and whispered, "He will teach you all you'll need, and remind you of who you are."

D.J. looked relieved, but continued to stare. "What is his name," he asked, "…my mortal father?"

"David. After the warrior poet."

D.J. nodded. "I like that." He stared again. "What did he choose? I mean – for his life's purpose?"

"To find his soul mate."

"I can't think of a better reason to live."

God hugged him, and sent him on his way.

David returned home from work and was greeted by Lindsey at the door. She was beaming and held her hands behind her back. He smiled, curiously, and kissed his wife. "What are you hiding?" he asked.

"A gift for you," she answered, playfully.

"A gift…for me?" He held out his hands. "Well?"

She kept her hands behind her back, and a mischievous smile covered her face. Tears formed in her sparkling eyes.

David chose persistence. "I can't have it now?"

She couldn't take it anymore. She pulled her arms out from behind her back and revealed absolutely nothing. He was baffled.

She wrapped her arms around him and kissed his neck. "In nine months," she whispered into his ear.

It only took a moment before it registered – before he hugged her tight. As if he might be hurting his child, though, he quickly pulled away and bent to kiss her belly. "Oh, Linds," he whimpered.

She pulled him to his feet. They embraced tightly and cried together.

The month's ticking off Lindsey's pregnancy were magical. They shared the joyous news with loved ones at Cappricio's Restaurant. And it didn't take long for David to spoil his wife something fierce. Night after night, while Simon lay on the floor, she took the couch and ate ice cream. David spent the time rubbing her feet.

Before long, David and a larger Lindsey picked out baby furniture and tiny clothes. They set up the baby's nursery, while family and friends gathered to inspect and nod their approvals.

They took the childbirth classes at the hospital.

And each night, as they lay in bed, both sets of hands never left her belly.

One random morning, Lindsey tried to shake David from his sleep. He was dead to the world. "Come on, Hon," she moaned. "You have to get up."

He mumbled something incoherent and rolled over. She leaned into his ear and whispered, "Wake up, Daddy. It's time."

He lurched up, and looked at his wife through squinted eyes. "It's time?" he squealed.

She smiled. "Yep. My water broke an hour ago. We better get going."

He jumped out of bed and searched frantically for everything they needed – periodically stopping to kiss her during the chaos. Leisurely, she slid out of bed and calmly got dressed.

He loaded the new caravan, helped her in and sped down the road toward the hospital. The whole time, she took deep breaths and held on for dear life.

Once inside the delivery room, she lied on her back, panting. A sheet covered her. Dressed in scrubs, David paced nervously. Doctor Lauermann entered and took a seat at the foot of the bed. Reaching a hand beneath the sheet, he nodded. "You're ten centimeters, Mom. It's time to start pushing."

David stayed at Lindsey's head. She crushed his hand with each push. He felt a mix of helplessness and respect for his wife.

"Here's the head," the doctor announced. "Just a couple more pushes."

David peeked down and saw his little prince's crown. Tears rolled down his face. A few pushes later, a baby's cry pierced the room. With the newborn in his hands, Doctor Lauermann announced, "Congratulations, you have a healthy baby boy."

David kissed Lindsey. She was exhausted but smiling. Doctor Lauermann cut the cord and placed the child on Lindsey's chest. "Okay, little guy," he whispered, "It's time to meet your Mom and Dad."

All three were crying. Between sobs, Lindsey told David, "Oh my God, Babe. He looks just like you. Let's name him David Jr."

David kissed her once more, and then kissed his newborn son. "Happy Birthday, D.J." he whimpered. "It's nice to finally meet you."

The hospital room was filled with flowers. Both families had visited the baby and were leaving. Though exhausted, Lindsey and David were grateful for the time alone with their child. Lindsey cradled the boy in her arms. They stared forever at the perfect, little gift. D.J. opened his eyes, yawned once and offered a slight smile. They laughed, joyously.

"He seems so happy," Lindsey said. "Do you think he knows something we don't?"

"Maybe he's just remembering where he came from." David kissed his son.

As a family, the three held each other tight.

~ VIII ~

At D.J.'s baptism, Jacob and Sarah were honored as Godparents. As the family left the church, Jacob grabbed David. "Thanks for asking Sarah and I to stand up for D.J. It means the world."

David patted his back. "It's actually nice to know that, God forbid, anything ever happened to Linds and I…"

"Well, that's not going to happen," Jacob interrupted. "I'm just grateful to play such an important role in the life of another child." He peered into David's eyes. "I want you to know, I'll always be there for your son."

David patted Jacob's back. "We know," he said. "That's why you were picked."

After the baptism party, David headed off to the beach for a quick run. Captain Eli was aboard *SERENDIPITY*. "Haven't seen you around here lately," the good Captain acknowledged.

David beamed. "Lindsey and I had a son. Nine pounds even."

"Fantastic! His name?"

"David Jr., or D.J." he said, proudly.

Captain Eli nodded. "Welcome to fatherhood."

"I didn't know you have children."

Captain Eli offered a wink. "Children are amazing. It doesn't matter how many you have. Each one shows you the world through a different set of eyes."

"I can imagine. Late at night, I just sit and stare at D.J." David couldn't wipe the grin from his face. "And he usually smiles back at me – a big smile like he wants to tell me a secret but can't find the words."

"Then he probably does. Some people believe we are closest to God at the beginning and end of our lives." He sighed heavy. "If only there was no past or future and everything were now."

David looked confused, but nodded just the same. As he started down the beach, Captain Eli called out, "Any resemblance to his father?"

"Spitting image," David yelled back. His words overflowed with pride. Captain Eli laughed aloud.

The months ticking away D.J.'s growth were even more magical. David and Lindsey took D.J. into their bed and bonded with him. Three winks later, they were at the mall handing the boy over to Santa for a holiday photo.

At Grandma's house, the entire family was playing with D.J. when the baby spoke his first word. "Dada."

"Very good, D.J.," Lindsey said. "Now say Mama. Ma...ma."

D.J. smiled and rambled on. "Da....da...da...da."

The entire family laughed. Everyone applauded. David turned to Lindsey. "Remember," he teased, "he said Dada first."

She giggled and punched him in the arm.

It seemed only a few more moons had come and gone before D.J. celebrated his first birthday. Lindsey helped the boy blow out his candle. David helped him jam both hands into the cake. Everyone laughed.

And while the boy grew, David and Lindsey spent every moment falling deeper in love with each other.

At night, they enjoyed the warmth and security of lying quietly in each other's arms. Soft music played in the background, while the dim light of flickering candles offered just enough light to reveal the contours of their naked bodies. While David stroked Lindsey's hair and offered the sweetest, most gentle kisses for her forehead, she stroked his broad chest and thanked God for bringing such a beautiful man into her life.

As the weeks turned into months, they talked for hours on end – about everything and nothing at all. Even when no words were spoken, both were completely content. Many nights, they engaged in hours of passionate love making before falling asleep from total exhaustion. Waking with smiles on their faces, they got dressed, grabbed D.J. and headed out the door – destination unknown. Though there was never silence, the radio was rarely turned on in the car. Lindsey's hand lay nestled in David's lap for the entire ride. They talked, laughed, joked, planned, kissed and usually drove to the beach. Hand-in-hand, they took long walks, while D.J. sat atop his father's shoulders and absorbed the wondrous world around him. Sometimes David and Lindsey stopped along the way to steal a kiss from each other. D.J. always laughed. On the ride home, they stopped off at the local ice cream shop to treat themselves to giant cones of chunky chocolate chip. While they ate, both counted off the minutes until bedtime. It was absolutely magical – rediscovering each other and falling in love again and again and again. It was the romance of a lifetime.

On the weekends, David normally awoke earlier than Lindsey to spend a few precious moments staring at her angelic face. He kissed her, gently. She stirred and cracked the cutest smile. With the world in the palm of his hand, he tiptoed out of the room and left her to her dreams of a joyful future.

D.J. awakened and called out from his crib. "Mama. Dada." David hurried to his son. He picked him up and whispered, "We have to keep quiet, big guy. Mommy deserves a morning to sleep in." After preparing a tray of eggs and coffee, David picked a wildflower from the yard and placed it into a small crystal vase. As D.J. settled back into his crib with a warm bottle, David snuck back into he and Lindsey's dark bedroom, placed the breakfast tray at her feet and lay beside her once again. He kissed her everywhere, inhaling the intoxicating scent of her love. When her eyes slowly opened, he gently rested himself atop her and kissed her with all the passion that made his heart ache. As she reached for him, he stopped her and offered the warm breakfast. She smiled and thanked him with her eyes. He returned the smile and shivered. The intensity in her eyes still gave him chills.

They snuggled on the couch and watched movies. They sat out on their porch and made out like two teenagers – eventually making love beneath the stars, their eyes never once leaving each other's gaze. And when neither could take anymore, David wrapped his love in a soft, fluffy robe and carried her off to bed where he held her for the night.

On weekday mornings, they'd awaken to music blaring in the background. As David reached over her for the fifth time to swat the snooze button, Lindsey chuckled aloud and realized that he needed more than the alarm clock. She kissed him – giving him the strength to take on the world. Lying atop of him, she whispered sweet nothings and her dreams for their future. A squeal traveled from across the hall "Mama!" D.J. was up. It was time to do the same. While David took his shower, she packed his lunch – including a small love letter. He got dressed, kissed his son and headed for the world that surrounded their dream. "Be careful and hurry back," she always said at the door, and sent him off to work with the sweetest kiss. She then took a seat at the computer and sent him an email, nothing elaborate – just something that would make him smile and keep his thoughts where they belonged; with her.

When they weren't together, David constantly daydreamed about Lindsey. No matter how much time passed, she did the same. Whether they hadn't yet experienced it, or wished to experience it together a dozen more times, their plans were mutual: Long, romantic walks along the beach, skinny-dipping at night, fancy dinners on the mainland, and nights at the theater where they could sit side-by-side and hold each other's hands. Rainy nights and late fees at the video rental store. Getaway weekends at a Bed & Breakfast up north, making out in darkened movie theaters, and playing with each other's feet beneath restaurant tables. Hiking and camping and sleeping beneath the stars out in the middle of nowhere-- where no one could hear their passionate screams. Hours of incredible lovemaking. David reading poetry to her, and Lindsey begging him to write more. Long showers together, preparing dinner for three, and lying in each other's arm – sharing their secrets and dreams, everything. Skiing in the winter, horseback riding in the fall, and other vacations away. Nostalgic afternoons of roller-skating, and nights out on the town – drinking and dancing their troubles away. A rock concert. Picking apples and pumpkins. Snowball fights in December, water balloon fights in July and buckets and buckets of laughter. Playing cards and listening to music together. Getaway lunches and late night snacks. Boating and sunsets and piggy back rides.

The list was endless and both understood that it would take a lifetime to fulfill – the best of it, costing more imagination than money.

They loved each other so much that their hearts actually ached. Neither could imagine being apart. Life was better than good. It was perfect.

Unity for Lindsey.

There is a moth that flutters in the stomach,
searching for that light of love...
for which it is so desperately attracted.
Once discovered,
a greater gift cannot be found.
Alas, two hearts beat to the rhythm of one,
beginning life's unpredictable waltz.
Together, taking the hand of the Lord,
they shall be led.
Forever placing each other before themselves,
their spirits glide across a ray of sunlight.
At times, the rain drowns out that gentle harmony,
causing one to stumble, the other; fall.
Yet, with understanding and simple forgiveness,
the music never stops.
Throughout the song, constant joy proves unrealistic,
but whether each step is smooth or awkward,
complete unity is all they will ever need.
As partners, their unconditional love-
shall dance into eternity...

~ IX ~

They tucked D.J. in for the night. The baby plucked the bottle from his mouth and muttered, "Mama. Dada." Chuckling, they kissed him and shut off the light. As they stepped out of the room, Lindsey stumbled and nearly fell to the floor. David caught her. "Linds, what's wrong?"

She was groggy. "I don't know. All of a sudden, I just feel so weak."

He helped her downstairs and on to the couch. "Lie down. Relax," he insisted. "Have you felt like this before?"

She was ashamed to admit it. "I've been feeling exhausted for the past month or so," she mumbled. "I don't know."

He was angry. "Why didn't you tell me?" He quickly quieted his tone. "We'll go see the doctor tomorrow."

She nodded, laid her head back and shut her eyes. He sat beside her, worried.

The doctor checked Lindsey. "It's probably just fatigue," he predicted, "with you running around after the baby, and all. But to be on the safe side, I've ordered a series of tests. Joan will be in to take some blood and urine." Doctor Nichols left. Nurse Joan entered and began extracting blood.

Four days later, while David fed D.J. in his high chair, Lindsey answered the phone. Her face turned from happiness to worry. David put down the baby's spoon. "What is it?" he asked.

She raised a finger for him to wait. Her face said it all. It wasn't good. He stood and swallowed hard. A few moments later, she hung up and turned to face him. She was reluctant to speak. "It was Doctor Nichols. He said the tests came back." She stopped.

He stepped to her. "And what?" Fear filled his eyes.

"My blood showed some abnormalities." Her voice broke up. "He wants to see us in his office tomorrow morning."

He grabbed her shoulders. "That's all he said?"

She nodded, but couldn't hold back the tears.

He put on his bravest face and shrugged. "It's probably nothing. Let's not worry until we have to. And whatever it is, we'll face it together, okay?"

They hugged.

Lindsey and David squirmed terribly in Doctor Nichols office. The physician was painfully stalling.

"Just tell us, please!" Lindsey blurted. Her nerves were shot.

With the most sorrowful expression, the doctor looked up and broke the dreadful news. "You have Leukemia, Lindsey. "

She felt ready to pass out.

"But it can be treated, right?" David asked through quivering lips.

Doctor Nichols shook his head, sadly. "David, right now, there is no cure, but…"

David collapsed back into his seat. He rubbed his head over and over. "Oh, dear God," he repeated. "Oh, dear God."

"Leukemia is a mysterious disease," the doctor explained. "For whatever reason, the white blood cells begin multiplying and start killing off the red cells. It's often hereditary, but in this case…" He stopped.

David and Lindsey were crushed. Definitions didn't help.

"The disease often goes into remission for long periods of time," he added, softly. "Some people live for years after being diagnosed."

Lindsey cried uncontrollably. David embraced his wife and tried to be strong. Doctor Nichols shook his head. He was disgusted. There was nothing he could do for the young couple. They returned home to face the living nightmare.

While David silently wept, he stroked Lindsey's hair until she fell asleep. After kissing her forehead, he checked in on D.J. The baby was sleeping peacefully in his crib, so he headed for the door.

He moped solemnly along North Beach until finally dropping to the sand on his knees. Clasping his hands tightly together, he looked toward the sky and negotiated with God. "Dear God," he pleaded, "Please don't take Lindsey from me – from us." He sobbed terribly. "I'll do anything. Just don't let her die."

With his head hung in desperation, he knelt in silence for a while. He looked back toward the sky. "Show me a sign, Father," he begged. "I need to know that everything's going to be…"

He felt a tap on his shoulder and jumped. Captain Eli was standing over him.

"Sorry to startle you, David. It looked like there was something wrong."

"Lindsey has Leukemia," David blurted.

Captain Eli took a seat in the sand, and placed his strong hand on David's shoulder. David waited for the man's wise words. Captain Eli said nothing. Instead, he stared out onto the dark horizon. David began to weep, uncontrollably. Captain Eli never removed his hand from David's shoulder. When he finally came up for air, David turned to his old friend. "I didn't ask for this," he whimpered. "This was not part of the plan."

"Some people live an entire lifetime in one moment, David. It's what you make of it." He looked hard into David's eyes. "Don't waste another moment."

The weeks that ticked off Lindsey's illness were the worse imaginable. As the seasons changed, the McClain and Wood families came together to support the young couple. As Lindsey rested, David took primary care of their son.

David held D.J. upright until the toddler could gain his own balance. As he finally let the boy go, D.J. took three quick steps and fell into Lindsey's arms. They were overjoyed. David applauded. Lindsey kissed the boy, but quickly asked that David take him. She felt very ill. David placed D.J. into the playpen.

Lindsey sighed. "I'm so happy I was here to see his first steps."

"You're not fighting this thing hard enough, Linds," David yelled. The anger was eating him alive. "It's like you're giving up."

"There's nothing to fight, David," she replied, gently. "And I'm not giving up. I've just placed it all in the hands of God."

David was beyond upset. "But He's not listening!" he screeched, and stormed out of the room.

Tears rolled down Lindsey's face – tears shed for her husband's pain and for the realization of all she'd miss in D.J.'s life. She thought about her boy's first day of school and the anxious look on his face when he stepped onto the big, yellow bus. She imagined the many report cards she'd never read, the new clothes he'd pick for his first date and the daffy smirk he'd wear after his first kiss. She wouldn't be there for his high school graduation or to offer her support throughout his college years. And her heart ached as she pictured him standing alone at his wedding when it was time for them to dance. Not playing Grandma for his children caused her entire body to shake. They were all being cheated. She wept harder than she'd wept her entire life.

David ended up on North Beach where the reality of Lindsey's impending death brought him to his knees. He was done negotiating with God and had reached anger. He felt betrayed. On bended knees, he looked toward heaven and screamed, "My whole life, I did everything I felt was right; everything I learned as being good. I worshipped you. I worked hard, and I've been good to people – treating them as I wanted to be treated." Enraged, he asked, "And this is what I get? I've waited my whole life to find someone to love and when I finally find her, you're going to take her away?"

He wept uncontrollably, reached his hands toward heaven and screeched, "I feel so alone now. Why? Why have you left me?"

Captain Eli appeared on the dark horizon and walked down the beach. As he approached, David looked up, his eyes leaking tears. The old man gestured toward the sand. David nodded. The seaman took a seat. After a moment of shared silence, David admitted, "I don't know what to do."

There was a long pause. "Then do nothing," Captain Eli whispered. "Just be."

"BE WHAT?" David lashed out. "BE HAPPY THAT MY WIFE'S DYING RIGHT BEFORE MY EYES WHILE THERE'S NOTHING I CAN DO ABOUT IT?"

Captain Eli didn't respond.

"I didn't choose for this to happen," David sobbed, "for Lindsey to get sick."

"Maybe this one wasn't your choice to make."

As much as it hurt, for whatever reason, it made sense. David looked at Captain Eli and for the first time, pondered the idea of acceptance. The two sat together in silence.

Exactly one month later, Emma entered Lindsey's hospital room with a large sack of takeout food. "All they had was..." Emma stopped when she noticed a stranger standing by her daughter's bedside. "Oh, hi," she muttered to the elderly, black man. She looked at Lindsey and shrugged. "I'm sorry. I didn't know you had company."

"That's alright," Captain Eli said. "I was just leaving." He grabbed Lindsey's hand and winked. "And I'll see you soon," he whispered.

Through the incredible pain, she smiled brightly.

Captain Eli grabbed the doorknob and tipped his hat to Emma. "Mrs. Wood."

Emma stood baffled. "Nice to meet you," she managed and watched as he disappeared behind the door. She quickly turned to Lindsey. "Who was that?"

"An old friend who came by to ease my mind about David."

Emma was still confused, but nodded and dismissed it. "David's on his way with the baby," she remembered aloud.

Lindsey felt ready for tears. "Oh Mom, he's not handling this well at all."

"I know. It's because he really loves you." The emotions began taking over and she hurried to finish. "We all do."

"And it's a mutual love that will never change," Lindsey confirmed. "That can't change." She smiled. "It's been promised."

Again, Emma stood surprised. "Promised?"

Just then, David and D.J. came though the door.

Lindsey dismissed Emma's question and turned on her smile. "And here's my boys now," she chirped, extending her arms. "Where are my kisses?"

David carried D.J. to his Mom. Big sloppy kisses were exchanged. After spending a moment with her son, Lindsey turned to Emma. "Mom, how about taking D.J. outside for a walk?"

Emma took the baby from her. "Come on, Grandma's angel. We're going to go pick some pretty flowers for Mommy, okay?"

D.J.'s innocent laughter stayed in the room a few seconds after they were gone.

David sat quietly by Lindsey's side and held her hand. "When did the contractor say he could start framing the house?" she finally asked, breaking the lengthy silence.

He looked at her, surprised that she would bring up such a trivial topic. "The house?" he asked.

She peered back at him, firmly, but didn't respond.

"He didn't," David answered. "And I couldn't care less if he ever starts."

"But I do," Lindsey declared, more adamantly than David had ever known her to be.

He was confused. "Linds, please."

"No, David. Promise me," she begged. She stared hard into his eyes. "Promise me that you'll finish our dream home."

By now, he was all choked up. "But…"

"No matter what happens, promise that you'll do it for D.J.," she added, "for all of us."

David began crying and placed his face into her shoulder. "I promise," he sobbed.

Lindsey took a turn for the worse. Both families were contacted and rushed to her side.

Emma sat at her daughter's bedside. Without words, they said goodbye. Emma was a wreck. Lindsey, however, was at peace. Emma kissed her little girl. "You should rest now," she said sorrowfully. "I'll be here when you get up." The last few words drifted on emotion. Emma was starting to lose it.

Lindsey smiled, compassionately. "Mama," she managed through the pain. "Tell Jacob that I need to talk to him."

Before drumming up the courage to leave, Emma grabbed Lindsey's face and kissed it. "I'll send him in," she whispered. "And never forget how much I love you."

Lindsey nodded. It would be impossible.

With Jacob at her bedside, Lindsey produced a folded piece of paper. Jacob was overwhelmed with grief. "Jake, I know this will be tough for you," she moaned, "but it's very important to me."

"Name it, Linds. Anything."

She handed him the paper. "When they lay me to rest, read this to those I love." There was a compassionate pause. She nodded. "Read it at my funeral."

As if it were too much to take, Jacob shook his head several times before he could read Lindsey's final message. Once done, he wiped his eyes and hugged his dying sister. He folded the paper and placed into his pocket. "Okay," he said. "I'll do it."

David and both the Wood and McClain families were gathered in the hallway, trying hard to support each other. The grief was overwhelming. Jacob came out of the room and gestured toward David. "She wants you," he said, "alone."

The rest of the family huddled in grief. David wiped his eyes and stepped into the room.

Lindsey was in great pain. It was time to say goodbye. He knelt by her bed and kissed her hand. "I'm here, Linds," he sobbed. "You're not alone."

She reached for his hand. "I know, David," she whispered. "And I never have been. None of us have."

He was moved by her spirituality. It was as if she knew something he didn't. She smiled. "And I need you to know that my life is complete."

He bowed his head and started to cry. She grabbed his arm and gently continued. "David, listen to me. We created a beautiful son together, and I will cherish your love for all eternity."

"I can't say goodbye, Linds," he stuttered.

She smiled even brighter. "You don't need to," she whispered, and then moaned once from the pain. "Just read to me, my love. I need your voice to soothe me now."

He fumbled in his pocket for a poem he'd written her. In a quivering voice, he read:

Beyond Death

You're the light that filters through the clouds
when days are dark and bleak;
an ancient wish upon a star,
the answer that I seek.

You're the song of doves and passing winds,
the music in my heart;
the calm before a rainstorm,
the hope where dreams can start.

You're the purest snow upon the hills,
the sparkle in my tears;
the sand dunes at the ocean,
a refuge from my fears.

You're the setting sun and smiling moon,
the one who steals my breath;
the woman who I vow to love
beyond that place called death.

He emerged from the poem to find Lindsey's eyes closed. She had smiled herself straight into an eternal sleep. He screamed out and cried uncontrollably. As family members came running through the door, he stroked his wife's hair and sobbed over the loss of a lifetime.

~ X ~

Lindsey met God in the cloud. She was the perfect picture of health and beamed with absolute joy. God opened His arms. She remembered everything and hurried to Him. They embraced.

"Welcome home, my child. How was your journey?"

"Inexplicably wonderful," she answered. "It seemed like it only lasted a moment, though."

God nodded. "Every life on earth – whether one year or a hundred – is over in the blink of an eye." There was a wonderful moment of silence. "You asked to experience love. Did you?" He asked.

"Oh yes!"

"Family? Friends? The miracle of motherhood?"

"Yes. All of it," she answered, solemnly.

God grabbed her by the shoulders. "Tell me what troubles your heart then?"

"I'm going to miss my son's life."

God smiled. "No," He said. "You will be there for D.J.'s first day of school and it is your presence he will feel when he steps onto the big, yellow bus. You'll be the first to see his report cards, the outfit he'll pick for his first date and the daffy smirk he'll wear after his first kiss. You'll have better than a front row seat for his high school graduation and it is your support that will help him get through his college studies."

Lindsey smelled rain. It was the scent of her joyful tears.

"I promise that your son will know you are with him on the day of his wedding. And as far as your grandchildren," God said, "you will meet them long before D.J. ever does."

Lindsey let her tears fall to the cloud beneath her. There was something more.

God searched her eyes. Without a word, He questioned her further.

"I never got to kiss my son goodbye," she explained.

He shook His beautiful head. "There is no such thing as goodbye.

174

You are connected to those you love for all time."

"I know that," she vowed. "I do. And I'm eternally grateful. But I need to kiss my son once more."

He peered into her face again, hugged her, and then gestured for her to leave. "Go in spirit then," He whispered. She took three steps when He called out, "But don't be too long. You no longer belong in that world."

It was dusk in D.J.'s nursery when Lindsey's shadow appeared on the wall. The baby looked straight ahead and reached with both hands. "Mama. Mama," he called out, excitedly.

Dressed in his dark, funeral suit, David was startled by the commotion and hurried into the room. Though he didn't see it, Lindsey's shadow remained. He lifted his son from the crib and comforted him. "It's okay, Buddy," he promised. "Daddy's here now." His voice turned to a whisper. "I know you miss your Mama. I do, too. But she's up in heaven now." The sobbing was getting heavy. "She's with the angels – where there's no more pain."

He held D.J. firmly in his arms and gazed into his son's eyes. D.J. smiled and touched his father's face.

David's sobbing was dreadful. "But we still have each other, right?" he whimpered. "Yep. It's just the two of us now. And do you want to know a secret, D.J.?"

The baby cooed.

"As much as you need me," he wept, "I need you more."

D.J. giggled and squirmed in his father's arms – reaching desperately to touch his mother's face.

David started out of the room with the baby in his arms. Just as they reached the door, D.J. looked over his Dad's shoulder, waved and said, "Bye, Bye, Mama."

On the wall, Lindsey's shadow blew her son a kiss.

Simon walked in and whimpered. As he glared at the shadow on the wall, his head tilted sideways. Lindsey's shadow placed its index finger to puckered lips for the dog to keep quiet. Simon lied down and kept his late master's secret.

At the funeral parlor, Lindsey floated in.

Suspended above reality in a dimension she no longer belonged, she peered down at her frozen shell. Friends knelt by the shiny pine casket, mumbling their brief prayers. "She looks good," they whispered to each other.

These comments alone were proof positive that she was dead. They couldn't hear her playful snickering. She floated closer, took a look at her mortal remains and cringed. A second look made her smile. "I always did look good in yellow," she muttered, playfully.

She took note of how David had honored her last wishes. A crucifix hung above her head in the casket's lid. Beside it, a photo of they and D.J. had been carefully placed. She smiled, kissed her index finger and placed it to D.J.'s smiling face.

Walking past several more mourners, who never noticed her presence, she proceeded over to the extravagant flower arrangements. She bent and read each card.

Her cherished husband stood with her mom and other family members in the receiving line. He looked so alone. Rivers of tears flowed straight from his shattered heart. She could feel his pain and without thinking, hurried to him. "David, don't cry for me," she pled. "My heart is filled with all of your love. I finally know peace and..." She stopped.

He stared straight ahead, his eyes locked on the woman who was once his wife. She kissed his cheek and again, whispered into ears that could never hear her. "I love you, and trust me, we'll be together again – before you know it."

She walked past her family and took a seat behind them in the second row. The funeral had just begun.

She scanned the growing crowd and noticed the funeral director pacing the floor, worrying whether the McClain family would satisfy the outstanding debt owed him. One well-dressed person after another entered the dark parlor. Most signed their names into a book that would never be read. Some dropped off envelopes containing donations to the Leukemia Society of America. All proceeded to the coffin to pay their last respects. With keen eyes, she escorted each one.

Neighbors, co-workers and friends she met along the way blessed themselves before her broken body and spoke to God. Some even spoke to her. Though no one realized it, she responded to each of them. With Lindsey as their escort, the mourners then proceeded to David. She stood right beside her husband as the heartfelt sympathies began. "I am so sorry for your loss," they said. "My deepest condolences."

Lindsey eavesdropped on several of the overlapping conversations. Mrs. Tuggle, an elderly and seemingly sweet soul, spoke in hushed tones to her friend. "They say Lindsey McClain was a spoiled brat," she whispered. "She never once wanted for anything." Her tone went even lower. "I don't know why we're crying for her."

Her friend, the town librarian, agreed. "I know. If we all could have been so lucky." The librarian looked at David. "She had everything," the old hag complained. "It's so unfair."

Both gossipmongers shook their heads in disgust. Lindsey bent down between them and screamed into their deaf ears. "AND I THOUGHT YOU WERE BOTH NICE!"

Lindsey bounced to a different grouping. Jill Rodrigues, her comical hairdresser, told funny stories of she and Lindsey's time together. Evan Manchester, her mailman, joined Jill in praising their fallen friend. This kind of talk shocked Lindsey as much as the old hens that gossiped.

It was the same throughout the room. People either praised her, or tore her to bits.

Captain Eli, seated in the back row, smiled at Lindsey. He was the only one who could see her. She returned the smile.

The pastor finally arrived, carrying the Paul Bearers in his wake. "Don't tell me David chose Coley Wilson as one of my Paul Bearers," Lindsey groaned, playfully.

Coley looked right through her with the same daffy smile he'd worn since she'd met him. She laughed.

The young priest quieted the small audience with Lindsey's

favorite prayer. The chorus of mourners recited, "Our Father, who art in heaven, hallowed be thy name. Thy kingdom come, thy will be done on earth as it is in heaven Give us this day, our daily bread and forgive us of our trespasses, as we forgive those who trespass against us. And lead us not into temptation. For thine is the kingdom, the power and the glory – now and forever. Amen."

At the conclusion of the prayer, the priest sighed. "To lose a loved one so young…"

His voice was droned out by grief. David only lifted his head when Jacob was called to deliver the eulogy.

Jacob stood and prepared to speak. Lindsey slid to the edge of her seat. She adored Jake.

"Lindsey Ann McClain is my sister," he began.

Seats squeaked with squirming behinds. Jacob was speaking in the present tense. Lindsey was the most surprised.

With a quivering voice, he went on. "To the world, Lindsey's life might have seemed insignificant."

The squeaking became louder. Lindsey cringed.

"But I am living proof that her life was anything but insignificant." He took a deep breath and explained. "My sister possessed the heart of a lion, yet she was unashamed to cry. She was always quick with the truth, but never harsh or condescending. She was one to voice her opinions, but never pass judgment. Capable of opening her gentle soul, she gracefully forgave the mistakes of others."

He stopped briefly to regain his composure. "Lindsey has encouraged and inspired me," he said, "yet taken credit for neither. She was a woman who reached and dreamed, never leaving anyone behind. Not sparing with her mercy, compassion or love, she often accepted less from others. And that's only what she meant to me."

Jacob pulled a folded piece of paper from his pocket. "Lindsey asked me to read this today and though the author is unknown, she said it was one of her favorites." He cleared his throat. "It is titled, In The End."

David was shocked from his paralyzing grief. He looked up at

Jacob, then quickly over at the casket. The tears poured freely. He shook his head and a smirk forced its way into the corner of his mouth. He looked back at the casket. "Author unknown, huh?" he mumbled under his breath. "You always could keep a secret."

Jacob's quivering voice read:

> Standing on the threshold of death,
> a lifetime of memories sweeps me away.
> My weary mind rewinds every second
> and my heart is filled with peace.
> I can't seem to recall the material objects
> which I once believed had brought me joy.
> The cars, the houses, the money-
> like grains of blowing sand,
> they have sifted through my fingers.
> As vivid as the moments we shared,
> I only see the faces of those I loved.
> I hear the laughter, even cherish the tears.
> Like counting sheep, the beautiful smiles
> of family and friends appear before me.
> But I am tired and it is time to rest.
> Awakening above my own wretched body,
> my spirit hovers in complete bliss.
> There is a sad echo of those who mourn,
> but still I must smile.
> For the only thing that ever mattered was love.
> As a blessing, I have known that love,
> both in giving and receiving
> and my life's work is done.
> Now it is time to go to my Father,
> but looking back one last time,
> I will take all of that love to Him.
> As it was in the beginning, in the end –
> there is only love.

The funeral parlor was drowning in sobs.

"I now know why my sister wanted to share this beautiful poem with everyone she loved," Jacob said. "It is impossible for a woman like my sister to die. For certain, she will be missed in the physical sense, but just looking around this room, it seems to me that from here on her spirit will simply live in the hearts of others."

Gesturing toward David, Jacob struggled to finish his eulogy of love. "When Lindsey's son D.J., and his children's children go forth into the world and brush against the lives of others." He paused to wipe his tears. "...it is my sister's touch that the world will feel." By now, he was sobbing heavy. "Lindsey Ann McClain is my sister. And I, for one, have been blessed among men." Jacob looked back at the casket. "'In The End,' Lindsey's chosen poem, is just a reminder for us – that someday we will all be together again."

David stared at his beloved wife's corpse. Through the tears, he smiled again. "Thank you," he secretly told her. "Thank you, my Love."

Lindsey beamed. She walked up to Jacob and tussled her little brother's hair. It never moved. "Thanks Jake," she said. "I owe you one. And this is from Miranda." She kissed her brother on the cheek. Jacob never felt it. "Oh Jake, if you could only see her. Miranda dances with angels now and she is so happy she radiates." She kissed him again. "And you'll be together sooner than you think."

Jacob never heard a word. Realizing this, Lindsey approached David, who was staring at the body in the casket. "Don't look there, my love," she whispered. "I'm not there anymore." She placed her hand on his chest. "Jacob's right. Look in here – inside your heart. It is the only place we don't ever have to leave." After a long pause, she promised, "And the pain that you feel now is only the intensity of the love that bonds us forever." She kissed him one last time and turned to leave.

Walking toward the light in the ceiling, she glanced back and saw Captain Eli seated in the back row. He was still smiling. She mouthed the words, "Thank You – for everything."

Captain Eli winked once and Lindsey was gone.

Lindsey returned to the cloud – to God. He hugged her.

"Thank you," she whispered.

God winked at her. "Worry no longer," He promised. "Not one of my children is ever alone." He pointed toward David, in all his grief, and whispered, "Just watch."

~ XI ~

David wandered the beach. For the first time in his life, he was clearly lost. As Captain Eli watched from a distance, Jacob parked his car at the marina and met his brother-in-law in the dunes.

"Mind if I walk with you?" Jacob asked.

David gestured it was okay, but said nothing.

"Sometimes it's better to get it out, David. It helped me heal."

"So you came here to tell me that time will heal this ache in my heart, right?" David's tone was bitter.

Jacob shook his head. "No. Not time," he said, and placed his hand on David's shoulder. "Love."

Pure rage stopped David in his tracks. "Wasn't it love that caused this pain?" he roared.

"True," Jacob admitted. "But it's also that same love that will reunite you and Linds some day. You have to believe that."

David started walking again. Jacob matched each step. David glared into his brother-in-law's eyes and hissed, "I do, huh?"

"It's like the poem said," Jacob answered. "In the end, there is only love."

Jacob had hit a nerve. David stopped, and with great cynicism, inquired further. "So you honestly think that you'll be with Miranda again?"

"David, to be honest, when Miranda first died I seriously considered committing suicide so that I could be with her – so that she didn't have to be alone."

David's face went flush. Jacob could have been a mind reader.

"But something deep inside my soul told me that suicide was the worse thing I could do – that my life wasn't mine to take, and that Miranda would never be alone. It was impossible."

David nodded. He felt the same.

"So to answer your question: I don't think I'll be with my daughter again. I know it. Haven't you ever felt someone enter a room before you saw them? We're more than just bones and blood."

He peered hard into David's eyes and went for broke. "Look, Albert Einstein was the most brilliant man to walk this earth. He said that we're energy and in our purest form, we'd be light. The good news is – energy can't die, David. It can only be transformed. So the only question left is – where do you believe it goes?"

David started crying. "So what do I do in the meantime? What do I do without Lindsey for the rest of my life?"

"Take good care of the gift she gave you."

Through the tears, David looked at Jacob and nodded. Jacob hugged him. "You're not alone, Brother," he promised. "Maybe it's time to open your heart again. You're surrounded with love."

A foghorn blew. Together, they searched for the sound. It came from the lighthouse. David wiped his eyes and nodded once more.

At dawn, David sought out Captain Eli at *SERENDIPTY*. As if he expected David's visit, the good captain nodded his usual greeting. "How are you?"

"The truth?" David shrugged. "I still feel like I'm standing in quicksand – like I'll never get out. I wish I could just close my eyes and sleep forever."

"That sounds like a permanent solution to a temporary problem."

"I wasn't talking about suicide," he clarified.

"Good," Captain Eli confirmed. "But either way, you wouldn't be there for your boy – would you? And he needs you."

David nodded, agreeably, but didn't respond.

"Just be careful of what you ask for."

"You're a very religious man, aren't you?" David asked.

Captain Eli grinned. "Not at all. I rely on faith. And I understand that we're only spirits having a human experience. Religion, on the other hand, is the selling of faith. If you have enough to sustain you, there's no need to buy more, right?"

David didn't answer.

Captain Eli forged on. "Stop seeing the world through your eyes. That's faith." He embellished. "My friend, the Lord doesn't take something without giving more in return."

David thought for a while. Captain Eli waited. David said, "You once told me that I could have whatever I wished, but when I prayed for Lindsey to get well – it didn't come true."

"True," the wise man interrupted. "Whatever you wish for your life, not someone else's."

David pondered this.

"From where you stand right now, David, what is it that you want most?"

"To be happy again."

"Then be happy again."

David looked at his mentor with disbelief.

"We don't do happy," the man explained. "We simply decide to be that way and we are. David, we can't always choose what happens, but we can choose what we think or feel about it. And, it's that attitude that dictates the lives we live."

David was finally showing signs of coming around. "You make it sound so easy," he whimpered.

"Because it is. Life is simple. We're the ones who mess it up." He offered a wink to drive the point home.

David was taking it all in when Captain Eli grabbed his shoulders, peered into his eyes and went for the kill. "David, every morning for the rest of your life, ask yourself, *Is this who I want to be today?*" He shrugged. "When you're that aware of the responsibility you have for your own life, every decision you make will take you one step closer to whatever it is you want. Perseverance will take care of the rest. But the catch is…" He stared deeply into David's eyes. "These choices can only apply to your life."

David grinned. "You would have made a great preacher."

"No. People don't listen to preachers," Captain Eli said, returning the grin. "They listen to friends."

David moved closer to Captain Eli and extended his hand. "Thank you, my friend – for everything."

"That's what I'm here for. You're going to be fine." He smiled. "The both of you."

David began crying. For the first time, they were tears of relief.

Captain Eli finished by whispering a secret. "Just remember three things: We can only do our best with the gifts God gives us. Acceptance is one of the straightest paths to peace. And don't be so serious." He grinned. "It's only life."

Captain Eli smiled, brightly. David nodded and returned it to him.

That night, on North Beach, David sat in the dunes alone. He wiped his eyes and looked toward the lighthouse for a long while. Adjusting his gaze to the stars, he whispered, "Linds, I love you with all my heart. I do. But I have to go on with my life now. For D.J.'s sake – for my sake. But if you ever feel lost or alone, let the light guide you back to me. I'm here."

"And so am I, my love," Lindsey whispered on the wind. "…for always."

David stood and walked home to his son.

Lindsey and David's dream home was built one year later on North Beach. Two Adirondack chairs, one big and one small, sat on a wrap-around porch that faced the lighthouse. Skylights located above the bedrooms glistened in the sun.

D.J. was two and a half. David was putting the finishing touches on a sandcastle he'd built for his son when the boy ran over and fell on it, crushing most of it. David shook his head and laughed. He picked up the boy and tossed him into the air a few times. As D.J. reached hysterics, David whistled for Simon. The dog approached with a leash in his mouth.

While David used his free hand to hold Simon's leash, he and D.J. walked hand-in-hand down the beach. Suddenly, a seagull landed at their feet. David braced for the worst. Curiously enough, though, Simon never flinched. Puzzled, David looked up to find Captain Eli slowly heading out of the marina in *SERENDIPITY*. All of Captain Eli's nets were loaded on the boat. It was going to be a long trip at sea.

Captain Eli stood on the bow, smiling. "I suppose there's hope for all of us," he yelled toward the shore.

David nodded and waved good-bye. The captain waved back, and then turned his body toward the sea before him – toward another journey filled with joy and pain.

David looked down at his little boy for a long while and smiled. Shielding his eyes from the sun's glare, he then looked into the bright sky. "Thank you, Lindsey," he whispered. "Thank you for my son."

He unleashed Simon and let him run free. As he and D.J. continued hand-in-hand down the beach toward the sunset, he glanced over at his convertible and then back to D.J. A giant, peaceful smile covered his face. In his mind, he recited a future poem for his boy.

ARE WE THERE YET?

Holding to a steady pace,
from the back seat came a voice.
In belief that life was one long race
and fate, a simple choice.

"Are we there yet?" was his main concern,
as he twisted in his seat.
And I felt the sorrow he would learn
for the trials he had to meet.

"A few more miles...a little while,"
though I knew the trip was long.
But in the mirror, beamed a smile,
for my word could not be wrong.

So we talked and laughed, we shared the ride
and in time he took the wheel.
Through the years, we traveled side-by-side,
to think, to hope and feel.

Then I turned to him – my tired voice,
"Are we there yet?" was my plea.
He grinned and said, "That's God's own choice!"
For at last, my boy could see.

It finally reached dusk. Of the two silhouettes that stood in the cloud, Lindsey breathed heavy and clasped both hands on her chest in a show of love.

God looked at her. "Do you see now?" he asked. "There is a perfect plan for everyone."

She shook her head. "I see and I am so very grateful, but..."

"But?"

"Did I fulfill my purpose?" she asked.

God wrapped His great arms around her. "You asked that your life would make a difference." He winked. "You made all the difference in the world." He smiled and then pointed down to David and D.J. "You introduced soul mates."

The End

Printed in the United States
1460900003B/103-126